A MESSAGE FROM THE PUBLISHER, BAILEY HUNTER

Happy New Year, fellow fiends!

This beauty kicks off our second season since our resurrection. So much has happened, and so much great fiction have been shared over the last twelve months.

The stories contained within the pages of this issue run the gamut from twisted fantasy to dark humor, and all tales are sure to leave a mark on your brain.

As always, we thank you for your continued support. Without you, there would be no us, and no venue for these wonderful words.

I am ever grateful for our Slush Slashers. It's been a challenging reading period for them all, and they each have powered through to bring you, dear reader, the crème de la crème. We are ever grateful for their sharp axes, and keen eyes.

A big thank you to our proof-reader/copy editor, **Nick Clements,** and the extra support from **Amelia Gorman** for making it all sparkle.

As always, we welcome your comments. They can be sent to us at: **info@darkrecessespress.com**

If you are interested in advertising with Dark Recesses Press, please feel free to reach out to us at: **info@darkrecessespress.com** for a size & rate sheet. Our prices are incredibly reasonable, starting at just $15 for a simple b/w business card size.

TABLE OF CONTENTS

DARK HOURS

by R. L. Meza ©2023

The problem with success is no one wants it to end, not if they have a choice. They'll force the golden goose to lay her eggs until she can no longer lift her head, and when the eggs are gone, the goose dead, they'll paint white eggs gold and play pretend, hoping no one will scratch at the surface to reveal the ordinary. But someone always does. True artistic genius can be mimicked, but not well. And not for long.

As the sole creator, animator, and voice actress of *Peck*—the nation's number one television series for nine seasons running—Iris Peck was extraordinary. Irreplaceable. There could never, would never, be another golden goose like her. But when the cancer she had beaten twice returned to claim her at sixty-five, Iris refused treatment to prolong her life, knowing her battered cells would not survive a third time.

The problem with Iris Peck was not the cancer; she was ready to die.

The problem was the network executives wouldn't let her.

+++

"What is that?" I crossed my arms, hugged them straitjacket-tight to my chest, pretending the shivering fit was a symptom of the room's icebox temperature, and not a reaction to the mass boxed in glass. Knowing damn well what *that* was, but needing Ethan,

with his bleached smile and tailored Italian suit, to tell me. "The doctor said she passed. Where is she, Ethan?"

He nodded at the box, the long cords trailing like leashes holding a complement of beeping machines at heel. His smile widened. Each tooth beckoned like a window, begging for someone with a backbone to pitch a stone through. My shoulders curled, sucking my chest inward; no backbone here, just a growing sense of unease. No good ever came from a smile like Ethan's.

"How?" I asked.

Like I needed it explained. Money, money is the key to everything.

"Iris Peck"—Ethan always used her full name, not *your boss* or *your mother*—"donated her body to science. We shuffled a few things around with the university; they're thrilled with the new library. It's all legal, mostly."

Like kids trading lunch items in the cafeteria.

I inched closer to the box, the brain suspended in fluid; fine wires snaked between the folds. It was only a part, I reassured myself—the cruelest part, but surely harmless without the whole. Disgust and outrage slipped like sand through my limp fingers, replaced by nagging impatience. "How long do you plan to keep her like this?"

"A few days," Ethan said. "Just until we get the finale. Season ten's almost finished."

The wave of relief I'd experienced after the doctor's phone call receded as the EEG machine sketched a new diagnosis. Iris Peck had been dead, but she was not now. "Where's the rest of her—the body?"

Ethan waved his hand at the black bag lying on a gurney against the back wall. Seeking a distraction from the brain, I tried to offset the horror of the machines' insistence—alive, *alive*—by picturing Iris's skull sawed, the hair I styled anchored to a cap of bone. Without the makeup I applied, the face below would be slack and colorless, like a dilapidated house stripped of paint. Visualizing Iris as a corpse was comforting.

Once people figure out who I am, they ask what it was like, working for an icon—a goddamn national treasure. Personal assistant to Iris Peck. If I had to sum up my experience in a word?

Painstaking.

Ask anyone, and they'd tell you Iris Peck was a stone-cold bitch, a real see-you-next-Tuesday. They'd say it with a note of pride in their tone, like they knew her personally. Like it was admirable, her going through Hollywood's entire stock of PAs, and then New York's, before finally settling on the one person born and raised to take her bullshit. The only assistant stupid and meek and needy enough to hold her tongue.

I would have given back every paycheck for a hint of love.

"Is she conscious?" I reached out to touch the glass. My fingers wilted, drew back. "Can she hear us?"

Ethan snorted. "Of course not."

"What's the chair for?" I pointed a chilled, quivering finger at the vacant seat beside the box.

"That, my dear, is where you come in."

+++

I woke with vague scraps of memory fluttering in my head—Ethan wanted my help with the show...something about audio...voice recordings. I'd refused. Iris Peck was dead, or should have been, and I was glad to be free of her. Only, this didn't feel like freedom.

I couldn't move.

It came back to me then, how I didn't resist, didn't kick or scream or rake Ethan's cheek with my nails. Just raised my hands, uttering useless questions. Whimpering pleas. I let him back me into a corner. And then he plunged the needle in, popping my consciousness like a balloon. Everything after was a blank.

While I shook my head, chuffing like a drugged horse, a balding man in a lab coat knelt before my chair. The strap belted around my forehead prevented me from watching as he yanked on my restraints, but I felt the burn at my wrists and ankles, like a warning.

Too late, I started to struggle.

"What are you doing?" The question leaked between my numb lips to form a puddle of vowels. *Waeruoing.* I tried again: "What's happening?"

"As I said before, we need your help." Ethan stood back, scrutinizing me as if he could peel back the ordinary with his eyes alone. Like, maybe if he looked hard enough, the seed of genius hiding under my plain features and whisper-soft speech would be revealed. Because no child of Iris Peck could be ordinary, not fully. "We really can't do this without you, Daisy. You're essential."

The man in the lab coat herded the machines with their long cords into an adjoining room I hadn't seen before; it would have been at my back when I entered, too distracted by the contents of the box to notice the window set opposite the chair. Behind the window, the lab coat moved like a great white fish in an aquarium filled with equipment.

The balding man returned with a computer tower. The door swung shut behind him, muting the machines. I watched from the corner of my eye as he positioned the tower between the brain box and the chair.

"What's he doing?" With my mind stuck on repeat, my mouth echoed my questions from before. "What's happening?"

My eyes darted left, right. I tensed in anticipation, heart pattering so fast I was sure it would explode. Why didn't I fight? Why wasn't I screaming now? Probably for the same reason I'd held a position countless others had walked away from.

Weakness. Cowardice.

Pathetic.

"Don't worry about Doctor Cabot," Ethan said. "You're in good hands. His procedure has been remarkably successful."

"In chimpanzees," Cabot said. A rattle followed, accompanied by squeaking wheels.

"What?" The mention of a procedure cut my echo down to a single word. *Doctor?* I pictured a tray of surgical instruments rolling closer—needles and clamps and scalpels. "What?"

Like a broken record.

A loud buzzing startled a breathless cry from my throat. Metal combed my scalp. A strand of hair dangled over my left eyebrow, parted, then fell. Doctor Cabot switched the clippers off.

"Ethan, please." As the doctor swabbed my scalp, I cycled through every pleading victim cliché I could think of, but Ethan didn't look up from his smart phone once.

The unmistakable whine of a bone saw released the screams locked in my chest. Ethan smirked down at something on his screen, waiting for the span of silence when I refilled my lungs to deliver a cliché of his own: "You can scream all you want. Nobody will hear you."

Because the room wasn't a laboratory or a surgical suite, I realized. Ethan dropped his phone into his pocket and exited, appearing on the window's opposite side. From the array of sound equipment, he retrieved a microphone.

We were in a recording studio.

The screen mounted above the window flared to life. *Peck* was playing, though the scene wasn't one I recognized. And I'd seen every episode.

This was new.

This was something else.

Something about the animation was off. Judging from the grin splitting Ethan's face, he hadn't noticed the difference yet. But Ethan hadn't spent a lifetime playing shadow to Iris Peck.

"What's wrong with it?" I couldn't pull my eyes from the screen. "What did you do?"

Ethan's grin faltered. "What do you mean?"

"It's too..." I squinted, fumbling for the words. A flick of Ethan's hand, and the bone saw fell silent. "Their faces are too smooth, like they're not quite human. And the colors..."

My stomach cartwheeled with a sickening flop. This wasn't new: the drippy movements; the discoloration, like putrefying meat; the way the eyes seemed to rock and sway, as if floating in a sea of skin. But I'd prevented those botched episodes from leaving Iris Peck's private studio, deleted all evidence before the network executives could lay their greedy hands on what she referred to as her "darkest hours".

Longs hours spent watching her chest rise and fall, wondering if I should ignore her orders and call an ambulance. Wondering if the invisible ichor, seeping from the mind of Iris Peck to infect her work, was contagious.

Genetic.

Was it incubating in the recesses of my brain, waiting for a tragedy or chemical imbalance to trigger its emergence? If Iris Peck—someone who had everything, who *was everything*—couldn't fight it, what chance did I have?

"You said she wasn't conscious." My voice, a reedy whistle.

"No, I said she couldn't hear you." Ethan turned his back to me and stared up at the screen. Maybe he could see it after all; maybe this was exactly what he and the other executives wanted. But would one more episode be enough to satisfy them? Was this the end?

Or a new direction.

"This episode was plucked straight from Iris Peck's brilliant mind," Ethan said, with the reverence of an acolyte. "We have the animation, the script.

"All we need is her voice."

+++

The doctor injected a mild anesthetic—enough to pacify without compromising my speech. And so, I remained awake for sawing of my skull, watched the invasion of wires and other mysterious mechanisms reflected in the window. Felt nothing, save for the faint, suppressed drumming of anxiety, like fingers tapping on a trapdoor buried miles underground.

When the doctor was finished, Ethan rolled a teleprompter into the room. "Read the first line," he said.

I meant to refuse, but my brain had other ideas. In a voice that could only be Iris Peck's, I snapped, "Ethan, you rotten cun—"

An electrical current lanced through me. Bones jittered in blankets of twitching muscle as my consciousness blinked off, then on again. As the tremors subsided, Ethan cradled my face in his hands; fingers dug into my cheekbones, my jaw. His eyes searched mine for someone else.

"Iris Peck," Ethan said, "I know you are accustomed to your demands being met, but that was before. I need you to listen to me now. You will read the lines as they appear on the screen. You will cooperate—collaborate—in the creation of a final episode, a finale for our show. If you do not…"

Ethan plucked a scalpel from the tray and nicked the tender skin beneath my eye. He contemplated the red slick on the blade's tip. And then his expression changed; the grin was back, wider now.

"Are you ready to record?"

+++

Daisy.

My vision blurred, doubling the text on the teleprompter. The brief pause prompted Ethan to spool his fingers—*read it again*—behind the window. I stared at him in confusion. Why interrupt the recording by calling my name if he didn't need anything? I tried to voice the question aloud, but my lips and tongue continued reading. The teleprompter switched to the next character's lines; the screen above the window queued up the corresponding scene. The voice came again—a whisper, thin and sharp as a razor.

Daisy. Keep your eyes on the lines. Don't look around.

I recognized the source of that hissed imperative; clipped orders had guided my actions since I was an infant. If I were stronger, smarter, perhaps I might've worked up the nerve to retaliate with one of the belated responses conjured by my mind after a day spent cowing to barked commands, reprimands, and—my least favorite—the wordless gestures. Snapping fingers. Dismissive waves. Come here, take this, get out my sight.

And the queen of unspoken language: the pointed finger.

That my mother could be speaking through me, using me like a ventriloquist dummy while simultaneously communicating inside my head, was a nightmare worse than having my skull sawed open. Iris Peck had breached my fortress, the walls I'd spent a lifetime building, pretending I was shutting her out when, really, she was sealing me in.

Don't try to speak aloud. Just think—

Leave me alone, Iris.

Good. Perfect.

Praise? Frowning, I straightened in my chair. Maybe it wasn't her. Maybe the doctor had wired something wrong, split my consciousness in two by mistake.

No, Daisy, it's me. I'm here. The warmth in her tone triggered the old, instinctual squirming. Iris Peck was both pit and pendulum. The public perception of her mood swings was tame compared to the real thing.

She was the split one, not me.

We don't have much time. Please, listen. I can't control your eyes, so when I tell you to, you have to close them. Don't look at the screens.

Why?

Words trickled from my mouth. Behind glass, Ethan and the doctor watched, listening to a one-sided, superficial conversation, while underneath...

Daisy, I know I wasn't the best—I wasn't a mother at all, really. I was a shell. I had to be. Perhaps that doesn't excuse the way I treated you—

Perhaps?

It doesn't. It doesn't excuse the way I treated you. I haven't been myself, since before you were born—

Wow.

No—damn it, Daisy.

Ah. There you are.

Long, long before you were born, Daisy. My first year of college. I was young, stupid; I needed money to pay tuition, and they needed subjects. I volunteered for testing—experiments.

Ethan's voice came through the speakers. "Too slow. Read it again, but put a little more *oomph* into 'bitch'."

My eyes strayed to the screen above the window. Colors bled from the paused scene like a stain, distorting the screen's clean black edges, tainting the surrounding white paint. I blinked, but the illusion persisted.

Because it's real. Iris's voice carved a track through my mind, impossible to ignore. *It snuck inside my mind and waited for years to show itself. It pretended to be something it wasn't. Medication, therapy—nothing worked. I was so afraid.*

I tried to imagine Iris Peck as a vulnerable being. I saw, instead, the orange army of prescription bottles advancing to hold the ground between us. I saw shattered glass, spilled drinks, trash bins overflowing with shredded paper. I saw a gangly teenager dragging her mother from sweat-sticky bedsheets to stand under an icy shower, too terrified to call for an ambulance because the girl knew she'd be punished, like last time and the time before.

And then the show came; Iris birthed it, loved it, raised it like the child she'd always wanted.

The show was a cage, Daisy. Holding it in was destroying me. Killing both of us.

No, Iris. That was all you.

I know...Daisy, I'm sorry.

I blinked back tears. I was losing my mind; that last bit proved it. Never once. Never *once* had I heard Iris Peck apologize. She wasn't wired for human emotions like regret.

Trapped in yet another situation where I had no control, I was trying to justify her abuse, explain it away to make myself feel better about staying. About never telling her, to her face, just how badly she'd screwed me up. But no dark fantasy of a traumatized mind could alter the truth: Iris Peck wasn't a victim; she was a monster.

I'm sorry, Daisy. I am.

I leveled my gaze at the teleprompter. A few more characters and the nightmare would be over. I could ignore her—the other me—until then.

+++

We were almost finished. Ethan had saved *Peck*'s main character for last, to give Iris and I time to adjust to our new optical/vocal partnership, perhaps. Iris's voice adapted to fit and fill the new personality; she contained multitudes, a hive of voices.

Not one sounded like the woman who'd raised me.

Daisy, please. The show was supposed to die with me. You can't let it get out.

I wasn't sure how we were still reading; the words on the teleprompter were no longer displayed in English. During the first three lines, the letters tipped like dominoes, rolling over to form a tangle of interlocking symbols. The pulsing light was giving me a headache.

As a stream of incomprehensible dialogue poured from my lips, Ethan came to join me. He stood with his back to me, staring up at the scene playing on the screen. He whispered something—a breathless whimper followed by a moan. When the doctor emerged to investigate the object of Ethan's focus, he too became transfixed. They stood together, necks craned, swaying slightly.

Like charmed cobras.

The voice of Iris's main character—her pride and joy, her favorite—tortured my taxed vocal cords. My tongue contorted, writhing to form the shape of those foreign words.

The screen of the teleprompter rippled. The lines broke ranks, words elongating toward the center, letters stretching and twisting like pulled taffy to form glassy fingers. Warmth trickled down my cheeks, too thick and sluggish to be tears. Energy crackled in the air of the recording studio, standing the hairs of my arms on end. I relaxed against my restraints.

Not long now.

Stupid child.

It seemed the other me was trying a new tactic, shedding the unfamiliar persona of loving mother for one with more influence: Boss Iris.

I tried to make you strong, to prepare you for what's coming by making you hard.

But you are weak.

You have always been weak.

You bent, cowered, quivered. Why do you think I pushed you away? To protect you. Fragile, sniveling thing. You were my Achilles' heel.

Of course my mind would revert to a saltier version of Iris; it was the side I knew best.

Look at his face. Listen to the noises he's making.

Against my better judgment, I allowed my eyes to drift to the reflection in the window. Ethan was slack-jawed, his face bathed in blood from the nose down. Dangling at his sides, his hands performed a ceaseless flurry of movements, weaving empty air into erratic patterns. Wisps of smoke drifted from his charred fingertips.

Now that he's had a taste of real power, do you think a finale will be enough?

I ignored her—me—and returned my eyes to the teleprompter. The alien words bubbled like hot tar on my tongue.

He'll never let you leave.

Then stop, I challenged. *It's your brain reading the lines, doing the voices. Just stop and let him cut me up, already.*

Laughter.

I would if I could, Daisy, believe me. But it's riding me too hard. You're the one in control. You have to close your eyes. Don't let me finish it, no matter what he does.

Be brave, Daisy.

For once in your miserable life.

Fight back.

+++

Before I closed my eyes, I saw the screen above the window melt and begin to run, not down the glass but through the air, toward Ethan. His meticulously combed hair lifted, wavering in the charged atmosphere. His head snapped back. Tanned skin dripped upwards from his face in perfectly round droplets, revealing glimpses of bone beneath.

Beside Ethan, the doctor babbled responses to the lines issuing from my mouth—a fervent exchange not unlike the *Praise God/Halleluiah* of a tent revival. He bent double. His hands hooked into claws. Arms windmilling, Doctor Cabot painted the room with scarlet arcs.

Ethan shuddered. His suit jacket sucked inward, as if his spine had developed a taste for fine Italian wool. From deep within the invagination, white noise hissed.

The fingers emerging from the teleprompter dragged forth a wrist. Symbols pulsated over the translucent hand with the come-hither temptation of a predator in an ocean trench. A second hand joined the first, followed by a third and fourth. Reaching, seeking, the hands seized Ethan by the shoulders. Spun-glass hooks pried at his shoulder blades, opening a static tunnel.

Three lines remained unspoken on the teleprompter; they flashed with violent urgency.

I squeezed my eyes shut. The flood of words dried up, replaced by the soft, wet whisper of shuffling flesh. Imagining the worst possible scenario, I thrashed in my restraints, waiting for the other me to chime in, to lend her spiteful commentary on my feeble escape attempt. In the absence of her criticism, I replayed my life's soundtrack—a compilation featuring every cruel remark, every snap and snarl, delivered by Iris Peck during her darkest hours.

Footsteps approached, lurching. Drag, thump, drag.

Scalpel or no, the thought of him—of *it*—touching me was repulsive. Blood thundered in my ears. I threw my weight sideways, desperate to gain distance.

Something shifted.

I risked a peek through my eyelids. Ethan's grin drifted into focus, teeth crammed between cracked lips in too many layers. I shrieked, pushing back in my seat, and the chair beneath me wobbled.

It wasn't bolted down.

Panting, I rocked in the seat.

Weak, weak, you're weak! WEAK, fucking WEAK, Daisy!

No.

The box was to my left; I went right, hurled my body away from Iris's brain, away from Ethan and the thing riding them both.

Metal legs knocked tile.

The chair tipped.

Good gir—

I was dimly aware of a ripping sensation, like a taproot tearing loose from the left side of my brain. The white noise screamed with me. The chair struck the floor, clattering; its right arm broke on contact. I wriggled, reached across to release my left wrist, groaning through gritted teeth as I loosened my restraints.

Liberated from the chair's embrace, I rose on shaky legs. The teleprompter had dissolved into a puddle; beyond it, the doctor lay in a red-striped heap. Ethan's progress was arrested, mid-step. Face frozen in a rictus of anguished ecstasy, he pirouetted slowly on the toe of one shoe. His outline stuttered on the fringe of visibility.

The static reached for me, for the brain box, seeking to repair the connection.

I attacked the box, the essence of Iris Peck, with all of the fury born from living in her shadow. Swinging the broken chair arm like a bat, I shattered her glass prison. I'm not proud of what followed, but it was necessary.

Sometimes forgiveness takes the shape of a battle cry.

I still carry that last, feral shriek with me, encased in a box in the forefront of my mind.

To remind me what I'm capable of.

R. L. Meza is an author of horror fiction. Her work has been published in Nightmare and Dark Matter Magazine.

Meza lives in a century-old Victorian house on the coast of northern California with her husband and the collection of strange animals they call family. Learn more at rlmeza.com, or follow her on Twitter @RL_Meza.

150 Words About . . .
WHO INVITED THEM (2022)

by James Newman ©2023

Adam and Margo are a young couple living in the Hollywood Hills. She traded dreams of indie-rock stardom for motherhood; he yearns to be a bigtime player in real estate or something.

Enter Tom and Sasha, who show up at a housewarming party Adam and Margo are throwing (mostly so Adam can mingle with important people, when he's not acting like a child any time a guest goes near his record collection).

Once the party's over, Adam and Margo can't get rid of the sexy strangers. Things get weirder as the night progresses, but maybe it's because of all the drugs and alcohol the foursome has consumed. Are Tom and Sasha just fun-loving folks who can't take a hint, or something more malevolent?

This one's a fun low-budget thriller – nothing that will set the genre on fire, but it doesn't wear out its welcome (see what I did there?). Recommended.

A TIMELESS TALE
(With Edits)

by Logan McConnell ©2023

The dwarf's execution proved popular. His public hanging was attended by most residents of the village. One of the few people not present was the man responsible for the dwarf's death: King Ky. He remained in his castle, listening to the murmurs and gasps of the crowd through the closed curtains of his tower window.

King Ky had known the dwarf, named Up, since birth. Up was recruited by Ky's father as an impromptu jester, allowed to stay in the castle so long as he created merriment for the king, who was otherwise immersed in the stoic duty of governing the land. Soon Ky was born, and by age five Ky considered the dwarf a valued companion.

Up, however, was not a dwarf. Not technically. With elongated arms, a thin head and stubby legs that bent in peculiar locations, his body was more a bric-a-brac of limbs from other lifetimes assembled to create a figure short in stature. "Dwarf" was his descriptor for lack of a better term, a placeholder until a more appropriate word could be coined.

Up entertained Ky by cartwheeling around the garden in winter and somersaulting among the marshes and moors in spring. The duo's favorite activity occurred below the castle in the vast, underground catacombs lit by torches. Up would disappear into the shadows closest to Ky, only to reappear far away at the end of the hall seconds later. The nimble dwarf could travel undetected, using shadows like an exclusive passage for his peculiar variation of peekaboo.

Among the adults, however, Up was best known for his sock puppet shows. He would put two stockings on his hands, and move his fingers like mouths, conjuring silly voices in a high pitch squeal. Up's mouth never moved, his lips relaxed and shut as the puppets conversed or bopped one another on their "heads", their energy seemingly independent of Up's volition.

By age eighteen, Ky prepared to replace his ailing father on the throne. Ky had aged into a young man, his father into an elderly ruler near death. Up, however, rcmained the same. No wrinkles, grayed hairs or diminished joints afflicted him, he pranced and hopped as he always had, immune to time.

Up's puppet shows continued, too. Ky allowed these performances out of nostalgia, though adulthood forced him to view these acts with a new perspective. The dialogue of the puppet shows was filled with innuendos and bawdy punch lines that bordered on cruel, even depraved. In private moments, King Ky would ask himself: had Up grown more uncouth over time, or had this side always been there, in front of him for years, content gone undetected by a child?

Soon Ky wed Queen El. The royal couple shared the castle and all was well. Ky and El conducted their duties without much thought to Up, he merely a gadfly within the massive castle. Over the years, the Queen grew acquainted with the jester, and witnessed Up's disappearance into dark, faraway corners, only to reappear seconds later beside her. This unnerved her greatly.

When she brought this to Ky's attention, he calmly explained that that was the dwarf's trick, a performance done as far back as he can remember.

"How does he do it?" she would ask him. "In all this time, have you ever asked yourself how that's possible?"

King Ky realized he had not.

The moment of El's breaking point occurred after a banquet celebrating the king's birthday. Up had behaved as usual, taking out his sock puppets to the delight of the audience. After the festivities, Ky accompanied his guests to the great hall for farewells while El retired for the night.

Alone in her bedchamber, a modest fireplace served as her only source of light. El removed her jewelry by the bureau when a sudden noise joined her in the room. She would later describe it as muffled, squeaky laughter. The room half in shadow, she became convinced that the dwarf was moving about undetected within his familiar darkness, watching her.

El lit a candle and walked to the darkest corner. She saw two beige stockings draped over an armchair, which she quickly recognized as the very same pair used by Up for his puppet shows. For a moment, the crackle of the fire ceased and the wind outside died, as if she had gone deaf, until one sock moved slightly to whisper, "Boo!"

She screamed until her husband and the night guards entered her room. Ky consoled El, holding her until she fell into a fitful, unpleasant sleep. The next morning, she pleaded with King Ky to dispose of the dwarf, that he was more than a nuisance. He was an insubordinate, vile creature. Her husband complied.

That day Up was arrested and formally charged with the crime of disloyalty to the crown, though the court understood this claim was unfounded. The king had simply outgrown his toy. Upon signing the decree for Up's execution, the guard peered down at the parchment and turned pale.

"My King," said the guard, "are you certain this is what you want? I... barely believe what I'm reading."

King Ky leaned forward in his throne, pressing both palms down on the armrest's intricate carvings. "Nobody is above loyalty to the crown, even if that someone is a beloved fixture of the castle. This crime cannot go unpunished. Proceed as ordered."

The guard bowed and departed.

Before noon, Up was hanged. The king resumed his usual duties. The castle adopted a quiet Ky had never before experienced, Up's cries and giggles no longer reverberating through the corridors. That evening, Ky found El in her bedroom, the windows shut, her head buried under blankets and pillows.

He sat down on the bed and rubbed her shoulders. "He's gone now, my love. Don't upset yourself with such an insignificant person." Ky bent down and kissed the back of her head. He got up to open the window and let the red sunset light the room. El pulled a pillow off her head, revealing a pallid color in her cheeks and bloodshot eyes.

"I feel ill," she whispered.

Ky stroked her hair. "Then rest, my love. You simply need a good night's sleep. Everything will be better tomorrow, I promise." He kissed her again then laid beside her. The two soon fell asleep. The next day, Ky rolled over to feel a nest of empty sheets, taking several minutes fumbling around in a half-sleep to realize El was not beside him. He rose, dressed, and arrived at the dining hall for breakfast, his wife nowhere to be found.

King Ky turned to the guard, standing by the entrance. "The Queen isn't here?" he asked.

The guard nodded. "That is correct, my King."

Ky rubbed his chin, sat down at the table, and picked at his food while remaining deep in thought. "It's not like her to disappear like this," he muttered to himself. His attention was broken when he caught, in his periphery, two servants exchanging anxious looks.

Ky gripped his fork, and slowly turned to the two. "And what, exactly, is that expression for?" Ky watched as both men began to sweat around their foreheads.

"We are simply concerned for you, my king," said one. "This has been a trying time for everyone, your grace."

"Trying?" said the king. "What's trying? The execution? What is so trying about that? We've done them before!"

One of the servants shifted side to side.

"You are correct, King," said the other. "Please forgive us, our hearts were well intended."

Ky's shoulders slacked. "Very well." He looked down at the food he barely ate, and found the hearty meal unappetizing. "That will be all for breakfast. Go and gather the court," he said to the servants. "Let us begin our daily meeting a bit early, yes?"

His servants bowed and assembled his coterie of advisers, confidants and scribes. They discussed taxes, the construction of a new courthouse, next month's festival, and other standard topics of such meetings.

The problem was, nobody behaved as their usual selves. His advisors barely spoke. Some of the most talkative in his crew were silent. And above all, they

each wore a fearful expression on their faces, like the servants at breakfast. Ky concluded something was stealing their attention, something everyone was privy to but him.

Ky slammed his fist. "Are any of you going to participate in government? Or do I no longer need your council?" The already palpable tension in the room solidified around the men, and everyone held their breath.

"My King," said a scribe, "while we all have blind faith in your judgment, we are rather..." he looked around at the others, "shocked by yesterday's execution. It was so unexpected and, well..." the man trailed off, lost for words.

Ky stood. "This kingdom is not going to cease its duties over the death of some obnoxious, worthless monster!" he shouted.

The men at the table gasped. The guard, the most stoic of the bunch, had dropped his jaw. Ky waved his hand at the table. "Get out! Go! Mourn for your freak, and get out of my sight." He sneered at the men as they shuffled away. "Not you!" he snapped at the guard. "You stay."

When the two were alone, Ky crossed his arms. "Bring me Queen El," he demanded.

The guard did not bow or nod. He simply remained standing, his eyes widening. "Th— that is impossible, my king."

"Do you know where she is?" Ky asked.

"Yes... and if you wish, I can take you to her," he offered.

Ky scratched his head, clicking his crown with the rings on his fingers. "Are you being disloyal to me?" he whispered. "I think I've proven yesterday the cost of disloyalty."

The guard started shaking, the bravery he so often displayed slipping away. The king waited. "Sir... I am loyal to you and only you. That is why I carried out the execution myself. Except, I don't believe I can bring the queen to you. Please, I insist, let me bring you to her."

King Ky paused to consider that this was the first moment in his life the loyal guard had failed to enact his request. This, on the same day his advisors were tight lipped, his servants on edge, and El missing. Ky pondered. He could no longer continue so out of sync with the castle. Something strange was happening, and to discover what exactly that was, he'd play along.

"Very well," said Ky. "Take me to Queen El."

The guard led Ky outside the castle and over to the stables. Ky pulled his cape around his shoulders to cover himself from a light rain that began to mist the air. The guard pulled his carriage around, and motioned for the king to step inside. Once settled in his seat, the guard departed into the village.

Ky had wandered these streets many times, sometimes in the royal carriage and other times on foot. Though he usually remained sequestered in his castle, the village was always familiar, navigated by the king with relative ease. That day, he found the environment had changed.

The buildings remained as he remembered, but the people seemed exhausted and distraught. Every person walked with downcast eyes, hardly expressing a bow as their king passed them by. Ky looked away from the carriage windows, gripped his hands together, and shut his eyes.

The carriage slowed as it approached the cemetery outside of town. Ky stuck his head out the window as they passed under the stone arch erected above the entrance gates, where skulls chiseled in the granite greeted all who passed through. The crunching sounds of the carriage wheels were drowned out by the blood draining from his face. Ky called out the guard's name.

"Almost there," the guard replied. Ky shifted in place as the guard pulled the reins to halt the horses. The king exited the carriage. They were parked before a mausoleum, one built in a plot reserved for royalty. Ky approached the mausoleum doors, and placed his hand over a bare plaque.

"We haven't had time to inscribe the name and date yet. The stonemason will do the job tomorrow, sir."

The king opened the mausoleum door, where a bitter chill wafted over his face. He shut the door, gripped the coffin's marble lid, and pressed it sideways. Ky saw El's hands first, resting on top of one another, then her neck, bruised in a shade of purple only obtained from the gallows, and finally the deceased queen's face, beautiful and dead.

Clammy sweat dripped down his neck. The putrid scent of decay moved through his nostrils until he held his breath, pressed his face into his hands, and screamed. The king screamed until all his energy was spent, collapsed on top of El, and cried in her lap.

"Psst"

Ky lifted his head. El's head was propped up, facing him.

"Hello Ky," said El, in Up's high-pitched voice.

Ky stammered.

"Oh, my king! Naughty of you to try and have me killed," continued Up's voice, through El, her jaw bobbing up and down like one of his sock puppets. "But, for old times' sake, let me sing you a song, since you look so glum. It goes like this:

I've wandered on through many worlds, and find Earth's people pleasant,
So, I made a home with you, the king, instead of with the peasants.

I watched you dullards move about, all thinking you wield power,
Unaware of this hard truth: control lies in the hours.

I, for one, can bend and alter, time itself with ease,

I move between the past and now, changing what I please.

The lives you live aren't set in stone, but actions on a script,
Words and deeds that I can change! You're puppets in my skits.

And so it goes, before my death, I changed the story thus:
Your decree read El, not Up, a fix without much fuss.

Last afternoon spent in El's room, you thought was with the queen,
But in that day I rearranged, you spent it all with me!

I loved the way you cared for me, suspecting none amiss,
I loved the way you stroked my hair, and gave a tender kiss!

I made it so that you recalled: the day this dwarf was dead,
All others lived my altered day, when Ky had lost his head!

Time's edit, though complex to you, is really jolly fun,
Consider this a final trick, my time with you is done.

You think as king you're special? You're just scribbles on my paper
But I'm the star, for in the cosmos, all humans are bit players!"

Up smiled with El's mouth, and leaned toward Ky with pursed lips. Ky recoiled, backed out through the mausoleum doors, then closed them shut. The king looked about, disoriented to discover it was night. What he thought had been minutes in the crypt must have been hours. The carriage was nowhere to be found. Ky was alone.

From the dark came whispers. "Bit player... bit player..."

The dirt around him shifted, bodies writhing out of their graves, the cemetery filled with animated corpses. Up, from somewhere, was making them move, his final puppet show, having the bodies sing to Ky as one chorus. "Bit player! Bit Player!" Ky kneeled to the ground, pressed his hands to his head, and screamed.

Behind him Up was grinning as he ascended slowly into the night sky, in search of another realm for his fun.

Logan McConnell is a health care worker and writer of quiet horror. His short stories are published in Coffin Bell, Diet Milk Magazine, Vanishing Point Magazine, The Crow's Quill and others. He is influenced by the works of Mary Shelley, Shirley Jackson and Thomas Ligotti. He lives with his boyfriend in Tennessee.

Twitter: @LMwriter91

A CANDID CHAT WITH DACRE STOKER

by Rick Hipson ©2023

As the great grandnephew of Bram Stoker, you might consider Dacre Stoker bona fide royalty within the world of dark and gothic culture. It certainly wouldn't be much of a stretch considering he oversees the Bram Stoker Estate and has made it his life's mission to unearth as many hidden artifacts and historical data available to be found regarding all things Bram Stoker.

A former teacher and Olympic level pentathlon coach, Dacre may have as much in common with Bram as anyone living today and easily embodies our closest link to Bram Stoker we are likely to find.

As we celebrate the tail end of the 125th anniversary of *Dracula's* publication, I was fortunate to have Dacre agree to sit down for a video chat to discuss the many incredible insights and previously unknown facts about our favourite and most iconic symbol of terror in horror history, *Dracula*.

Thanks so much for sitting down with me, Dacre. I just finished reading your book *Stoker on Stoker*, and was fascinated to learn your great granduncle, Bram, didn't start writing books until he was about forty-five, not even twenty years before his early passing which, even for back then, was still a pretty

young age to pass away by. And please correct me if I'm wrong, but I believe *Dracula* **was Bram's fourth or fifth novel?**

You know, it's difficult to answer that question because his early novels, he's had different editions of them. Some of them were serialized. Let's just say it's somewhere between fourth and fifth because it's not an easy count. It's not as simple as it would be today.

And most recently, we now have the most annotated edition ever of Dracula you've published through Hellbound Publishing. What can you tell us about this book?

This edition actually shows in grayscale in the type font all of the words, the thirty thousand plus or minus words, that Bram was asked by his publisher to extract from the original manuscript.

What I was lucky enough to use to create that was, I think, a sixth printing of *Dracula*. You see, Bram has two great grandsons still alive. They're in their late 70's, one early 80's, and they have some of the cool stuff. Some of the things they've donated to libraries, some they've sold to libraries, but they've also kept some really interesting pieces, and one of them is this sixth edition of *Dracula* that Bram was handed by his publisher, and they said, "Use this to take out 30,000 words." Now, in our day, Rick, they'd just be on your computer, and you'd just go and do strikethrough or something.

Bram did exactly the same thing with the sixth edition of *Dracula* with a pencil.

What a massive undertaking that must have been.

So, what you see is lines crossed out, whole paragraphs or sometimes pages with a square around it, and an x in pencil, but when he actually got intricate and took out

very specific passages, sometimes he had to add a few words to bridge, to make sense of what he was taking out. That's one of the elements of this brand new 125th anniversary annotated edition of *Dracula* is you see the grayscale of what was taken out. In a different font you see the bridge words he put in. You also see references from the *Dracula* notes that he either put in or took out, and you also see from the typed script. The very last thing that he had in his hands that was typed up and handed to his publisher what was either taken out or put back in at that stage as well. It's an interesting study because, back to your original point, this whole quick, easy read, there's more to it, obviously, back in the day.

(The abridged treatment) is for the 1901 edition, and what Bram's publisher was getting at was this book has now sold well in its hardcover form, four hundred and eighty-five some odd pages, but now we want to really get it out to mass market much like they do today with your trade paperbacks. But what Bram was asked to do was take out anything that might be too complicated for people to understand. You'll see any references to Shakespeare, for instance, and there was a lot of them. Any references to serious deep sciences or anything that's fairly complicated he had to take out. And I'm sure it drove Bram a little crazy because all the studying that I've done and comparing notes with other researchers, Bram loved to insert that stuff; the ideas of the day, the sciences of the day. Mesmerism, spiritualism, phrenology, all this stuff. Well, a lot of that was removed for the first paperback abridged edition.

That must have been so frustrating for Bram to do, especially when you know he essentially spent seven years writing this book and the amount of meticulous research he put into this was incredible. By example, to your knowledge as well as anybody's knowledge it seems Bram never stepped foot into Transylvania, yet, he immersed himself in the research so heavily you would think he had been one of the locals the way he described it and how the characters of the region were depicted, which to me is pretty mind boggling.

It's telling, Rick, and now that you're in the know having read that, here's how I sum it up for your Dark Recesses readers. You've got Bram Stoker, one of seven children, with two sisters who were artists, not just painting and sculpting and stuff. But he's got three brothers—my great-grandfather being one of the scientists in the family—being medical guys. Another brother, Tom, being a career civil servant. And here is Bram: childhood illness, seven years an invalid.

Something weird happened. We don't really know what, and he emerged from that to go and become what I believe is probably one of those awkward teenagers that has a fast growth spurt. But he also had an interesting time socializing as a teenager, as he's come out of this seven-year sarcophagus, and he's now got to enter life and write his exams to get into Trinity, and he does and he passes them well. He becomes an athlete, becomes a champion athlete, and he grows into himself, but as he grows into himself, he is what I would imagine, having been a teacher and I look at people that I have taught and coached, *What's their operating system?* You know, it's like his IOS. This, what is it? And I think Bram was about fifty-fifty an analytical detail-oriented person who became the clerk, the Petty Sessions Legal Department; became the inspector of all clerks all over Ireland and wrote a legal manual for all the clerks in Ireland. A very detail-oriented guy, but then there was the dreamer. There was the writer, the guy who actually drew pictures and got awards as a kid; the guy who loved the theatre, the escapism of your imagination. You've got both of those things in Bram's brain almost battling against each other for supremacy. What is he going to be when he grows up? And in an interesting way, even though he excelled at Trinity, he was the head of the Philosophical Society, the Historical; he had a Masters in Maths. There's that detail side.

As you know from *Stoker on Stoker*, I was lucky to find Bram Stoker's lost journal and publish it with a fellow Canadian, Elizabeth Miller, from the University of Toronto, which gave us a look into exactly the Bram Stoker I'm describing now. This guy struggling to become a writer but also very interested in social concerns as he was growing up.

It seems you're not so far removed from Bram as far your own internal operating system goes. I mean, the way you describe Cruden Bay, formerly Port Erroll, in *Stoker on Stoker,* I can picture the inspiration Bram would've gotten not just from the scenery but from the isolation as well. It was fascinating to read about other people's memories of Bram and this wild man out there, with his beard and his walking stick and this long cloak blowing behind. No doubt that must have fed into the lore of *Dracula* when Bram all but became possessed by the perspective of this rebellious devil as he's perched upon the shore like a bat, screaming at the sea. It kind of begs the question: was this a man turned insane by his own makings? Or was this the work of a man, as you allude to in *Stoker on Stoker*, who was so effective of a method actor that he was able to walk with these devils and these monsters in this isolated place to make it all too easy to appear as if he had gone mad. In a sense, maybe it was the sanest thing Bram did for himself. Maybe that's what kept him sane.

You and I, it's becoming obvious that we think a lot alike. The insight you just revealed is almost word for word what I have gathered and taken and shared with fellow author, Dr. Leverett Butts. We are about halfway through working on a fictional story of Bram Stoker writing *Dracula* during the one summer, possibly two summers that he was writing *Dracula* while in Cruden Bay, Scotland. As you were talking about, and I don't want to give spoilers away, but during a possible descent into madness and how he was handling that, how his family and people around him handled that, and what went on.

I understand in Cruden Bay, Slains Castle was part of the land once owned by the Earl of Erroll. Did Bram visit this castle as part of his research for Castle Dracula?

Even though Mike Sheppard and I found no record of Bram Stoker actually going in, we are convinced that Bram Stoker was in (Slains Castle) at least once, and we are convinced as Bram described in chapter two, Jonathan Harker's arrival at Castle Dracula, walking up the steps, going to the front door with no knocker needed at Slains Castle, was welcomed in by the Count—in chapter two, as you read that welcoming statement—opens the door and goes through another door into a hallway, into an octagonal room with no windows to the outside lit by a single lamp. Bram is describing his exact footsteps as he walked into Slains Castle in exactly the same way.

That's incredible.

I gave this presentation with Mike by my side in the Kilmarnock Arms Hotel a couple of years ago, and a man stood up in the back of the Kilmarnock Arms dining room when we gave this speech and he said, "I have that lamp."

Wow, no kidding?

That's how realistic this stuff is, Rick, that I do. I go in these places, never know exactly what I'm finding, but when you go to places like Transylvania and Elite Tours or Cruden Bay, Scotland or Whitby, you find things. You find the right people like

Mike Sheppard or others that have insight. I bring a little information to the table, they have information; we put it together. It just goes on and on.

I'm amazed by how much there is left to learn and uncover about Dracula and the man who created him.

(Regarding the 125th anniversary edition of *Dracula*) I want you to do one more quick thing. Hold up that *Dracula* that Lynne Hansen did the cover for.

Sure thing. (Holds up the book.)

Look at it closely. Here's your host participation time. What is that a picture of right there? What do you think it's a picture of?

Well, I would've guessed before it was the castle from Cruden Bay, Slains Castle. Either that or it's

Bran Castle which had more to do with Bram's exterior depiction of Castle Dracula.

Okay, now look at the person walking into that castle. Bottom right-hand side. What do you think that represents?

Originally, I thought it must be Jonathan Harker, but I'm now thinking it's Bram overlooking the castle getting inspired to tell the story of Dracula.

Okay, man, you just hit a center ten, buddy, on both of these things. This is the mystery that Lynne and I wanted to create. Never before has a picture of Slains Castle in its heyday, the way it looked like when Bram was there, appeared on a cover of *Dracula*. And that little person down below by your fingertips is supposed to look like both Jonathan Harker and Bram Stoker. It's what a theatre manager would be wearing walking along the street with the bowler hat on.

Bram would have loved this attention to detail, I'm sure.

Dracula's castle in the novel is a merger of the internal floor plan of (Slains Castle). The inside of Bram's Dracula's castle is Slains Castle. The exterior is, just as you said, Bran Castle, which is in Brașov, Transylvania.

Coming back to the beginning of our chat, Bram Stoker the visual guy, needed to look at a sketch of a castle in Transylvania as he wrote the description of the exterior, but he placed it four hundred miles to the northeast of Transylvania, in a location very near the Borgo Pass. Now to really bring this all together, again, pieces of a puzzle, Rick, one of the books in the London Library—there was two of them he had used for his resource—has accurate maps of Transylvania in it. Both of them have little lines on the edges of longitude and latitude. Bram's notes in the Rosenbach Museum have a reference to 47 East, 25 ¾ West, where the River Sereth runs into Bistritza at Fundu. All of this helped me and also this researcher Hans de Roos, who originally discovered all this, pinpoint exactly where Bram Stoker planned to place that climatic battle at the end of the novel, as the band of heroes are moving in on the gypsies who are protecting the Count in the leiter wagon, in his crate, just before the sun goes down and they escape into his castle up on top of Mount Izvorul

Wow, gotta love it when a puzzle comes together.

It's the location of the castle. Spoiler alert: There is no castle there. I've been there with my son. It's an extinct volcano, which plays into the story, but he merged these other two castles for what he needed to be the perfect castle on top of this mountain.

The insight that went into that is incredible.

Yeah, and that's Bram. And this is Dacre Stoker, his great grandnephew explaining to you part of Bram's process for one of the coolest endings in the story. And to really finish this podcast off with a bang, the original ending of *Dracula* that I discovered out in Seattle - Paul Allen Estate owns this original typescript, and this is going to appear in my upcoming annotated *Dracula* with Robert Bisang - was edited out. Crossed out. You can see it plain as day. There was a volcanic eruption right after the Count crumbled into dust after the bowie knife went into his heart. Only Bram Stoker would be that detail-oriented that if he was planning a volcanic eruption, by God, he was going to make sure the castle was sitting on a volcano. And Mt Isvorol, at forty-seven and twenty-five and three quarter latitude, was an extinct volcano.

Dacre, it was an absolute honor and pleasure to chat with you. I do hope we can do it again. Thank you so much and long live the Count.

To experience the full, unabridged interview, visit: Dark Bites YouTube Interview: "**You Never Knew THIS About Dracula (With Dacre Stoker)**"

THE YOUNG WOMAN WHO LIVED UP THE LANE

by Jay Seate ©2023

Just outside the small town where Richard briefly worked as a young man lay a winding rural road with a breathtaking view. Danielle, his wife of thirty years, viewed this journey with a quiet tolerance. Happenstance had brought them together all that time ago when Danielle and her family were passing through the region on vacation. Love at first sight, one might call it. He left his menial job and followed Danielle to the city where he found not only her but opportunity. They married, built a life together, and prospered.

Thomas Wolfe wrote, *you can never go home again*, but Richard *had* returned to the place that, up until Danielle, once provided nourishment of sorts. "I used to know someone who lived out this way," he told his wife as they rode beyond the town proper along a picturesque winding road dressed on either side by aspen and pine trees.

Danielle leaned back into the headrest as the stream of treetops placidly swam by. "A pilgrimage to Richard's past," she offered just for something to say. This trip was no more to her than a quaint indulgence, but if Richard needed a nostalgic trip down memory lane, it wouldn't have been fair not to indulge him.

A small bake stand suddenly appeared along the route next to an overgrown turnoff. There was just enough safe space to slow down and stop if one chose to. Richard chose to.

What?" Danielle asked.

"I can't believe this little enterprise still exists."

The couple sat for a moment. *Was he really going to get out and buy something?*

"You want to stretch your legs, Danny?"

"I'll sit this one out."

"I'll just be a minute."

Richard got out and approached the stand. It was manned by a young woman. Her lips displayed a Mona Lisa smile. Making eye contact, a touch of the familiar unsteadied him. A momentary flashback took hold and then passed. He felt like a fool, but the lady didn't react to his mid-fifties swoon.

"The resemblance is incredible," he finally said. "Do you live up this lane?"

"I do."

"You must be the daughter of someone I use to know. Your mother… we…she used to sell trinkets and baked goods."

"And I still do."

+++

Marcy had a gift, a way of knowing things about people—their secrets, their longings, their regrets. All those elements were in *her* makeup as well. But today was unique from other days because a mission needed to be accomplished. One long overdue. Her freshly baked cookies were ready to be carried down to the roadside. It was to be a day indulgently drenched in nostalgia.

Living on the outskirts of a small town and being homeschooled, the loss of her parents at a young age left her in a quandary. She'd been left property and money, but not wise to the ways of the world. During this rather aimless period, she continued to bake and carry her goods down the lane for something to do rather than because of need.

Then she met someone—a boy.

In the yellow haze of a late spring afternoon he stopped and bought a bag of almond cookies. Then he came back the next day and the day after that. The boy was soon spending more time at Marcy's than in his small apartment over a garage where he worked. Before long she was providing meals along with herself, giving her a sense of purpose.

The twosome walked barefoot through meadows her hand in his, breathing the sweetness of the grass, sharing experiences concerning young love and what it could blossom into. It seemed an idyllic romance straight out of a fairytale. Nothing was said about marriage, but Marcy believed she could see the future, her life laid out before her. They would be married one day. In spite of his restless spirit, she looked

enchanted, people said, like a woman who could talk to fairies.

Small towns love their stories of love, hate, and scandal as much as the preserves they put up in glass jars to be picked off a shelf when a good tale needs to be told around a dinner table. So what transpired up the lane played well. On a day when foreboding winds heralded the coming of autumn Marcy's penchant for 'knowing things' apparently let her down. Her lover was gone like the proverbial wind. He could have told her, but he didn't. Just met someone else it was rumored. Packed his bag and hauled ass without so much as a goodbye. A girl who'd lost her parents too soon left behind. He had no ties here after all some said, except for Marcy.

Yes. Marcy. A young man had opened a door filling a wounded spot on her soul only to slam it shut leaving a space emptier than ever, shattering the mirror on Marcy's fantasy. A hopelessness descended like a heavy cloak leaving her in a cold empty place where dreams go to die. It was as if she had been jilted at the alter leaving an indelible hard rock inside where her heart used to be.

No one saw Marcy for some time afterwards, not even at her little stand. In town she became somewhat of a mystery living in an inherited old farm house with whatever ghosts might keep her company.

+++

Danielle was drifting off when Richard opened the car door. "Have a nice chat?" she asked her husband.

He seated himself before answering. "I used to buy cookies from the same stand."

"Over thirty years ago?"

"Amazing how some things never seem to change."

"Just like your little town. Only the advertising is different, you said."

"Amazing," he said again looking at Danielle as if he'd suffered sun stroke.

"You okay?"

"That girl is the spitting image—"

"So you have some skeletons in your closet after all?" Danielle offered, a casual smirk quivering at the corners of her mouth.

"Not skeletons. Just—anyway, I got some almond cookies. They're delicious. Try one." He waved a sack in her direction.

"No thanks. I'd rather look forward to a nice dinner somewhere."

"Suit yourself." Richard reached in the bag and helped himself.

They drove on a narrow blacktop running east-west. Twilight was quickly overtaking the landscape. Suddenly their vehicle swerved. Danielle looked at Richard. A horrible grimace distorted his face, then agonizing words, "Oh Christ!" One of Richard's hands left the steering wheel and went to his chest. The other hand tried to maintain control of the speeding death trap. At 50 MPH, the wheels lost purchase with asphalt. Veering off the road, it flipped on one side, rolled over, and came to rest with a crashing thud at the base of a tree.

There were no further cries. There were no further screams. The combined restraints of seat belts and safety bags were not enough to keep the couple from hurtling forward into the steering wheel and dash respectively. Danielle's chest cavity collapsed on impact and all cardiac activity ceased. Ricard's neck was broken.

There was nothing to be done when the authorities arrived except to call ambulances, extract the bodies from the wreckage, and fill out endless forms.

"What do you figure?" an EMT ask the coroner. "A stroke at the wheel?"

"Probably. We'll see what the autopsy gives us."

"Might have choked on a cookie. There was a bag of them in the car."

+++

When arsenic was detected in the male's body, it fell on the shoulders of a local sheriff to investigate the movements of the couple prior to their demise. A convenience store attendant remembered the man getting gas and some bottled water. "The guy mentioned he used to live here and asked if I knew a woman called Marcy who lived on the edge of town," he told Sheriff Decker. "Said she use to sell stuff along the road. Guess he was talking about the old fallin' down stand west of town that should have been scraped away along with the boarded up joint up the lane."

Decker knew the history: A naïve woman in a secluded house. A lover lost to another, disappearing inside herself over the loss of romance, the pain of betrayal. A rope thrown over a beam. A body found weeks later dangling from the kitchen ceiling. The woman who'd once possessed a special look of absolute trust and kindness creating her own horror story. Romeo and Juliet it wasn't.

Over thirty years ago.

He drove out to the location where a few withered boards marked the remnants of a fruit stand long abandoned. As his patrol car climbed the weed infested lane, he wondered what he was looking for while at the same time drawn by the unknown, fed by sordid tales about the young woman who used to live up the lane.

The house, although as bleak as an isolated property with a sordid past can look, seemed to stand expectantly. It was dilapidated, long unused, dying, if not already dead. Most of its paint had peeled and turned a dingy gray giving the appearance of scaly skin. Spider webs of cracked glass crawled along its windowpanes. A remaining shutter hung askew from a broken hinge. Some of the gutters around the eaves drooped loosely, bent and rusted, having long since lost their ability to catch water. And yet, the house had a hypnotizing quality as if wanting to relive its past, a place to shut out the world and shut secrets in. "A real fixer-upper," Decker mumbled.

Once upon a time, this had been a happy house, he imagined, before the people in it started dying. He wondered himself why the place hadn't been torn down, revitalized, or developed somehow. Maybe something about it frightened prospective buyers away.

The main door stood slightly ajar. The remnants of red paint darkened to the color of dried blood still remained. Its hinges squealed as Decker entered. He kept the stolid statement, "Police. Anybody here?" to himself. *Let sleeping dogs lie, for now.*

He drew his revolver, feeling a bit silly for doing so, as he slowly, carefully moved about the main room. The interior seemed barren at first. He reflected on what had happened within this house, absorbed the current aura, and listened. Was it the scurrying of mice, or whispering voices wanting to be heard? He wondered if the sounds kept most thrill-seekers away. With the exception of some graffiti and a living room light fixture ripped from the ceiling, there were few signs of trespass. Empty candy wrappers were scattered about, but neither vagrants nor horny teenagers would want to tarry here for long.

What was he feeling exactly—an air of people and times long gone? Or maybe more. He opened every available door before proceeding to a large kitchen. Countertops and cupboards covered by decades of dust and abandoned cobwebs placidly greeted him. Nothing unusual. Except for one illogical scenario: a recently used cookie sheet

with the presence of a twisted knot still fashioned around the beam. He suddenly felt like a character inside a horror movie trapped into playing the part of an ill-equipped lawman from the sticks. His head felt like a haunted house filled with hallucinations imagining the squeak of the rope swinging to and fro, apparitional movement in dark corners, the rustling of something unnatural, all suggesting he should be anyplace but here. He'd heard the theory about how the emotional imprint of tragic events could linger in a place where they occurred. Memories of death. Something gone and yet not gone. A recalled passage from some long ago story or poem tickled the funny monkey in his brain: *And so, it is said, you are haunted? My friend, we are haunted all.*

rested on top of a dusty table. And one more thing: a bottle of arsenic stood nearby.

Evidence? A prank turned deadly?

There were no smudges, just an open glass bottle covered with the same layer of time that only the cookie sheet escaped. The sheriff stooped down and sniffed. The almond smell made him lightheaded. He took a step back and leaned against a counter knocking over a bottle, the clatter echoing around the room. He absentmindedly scratched his forehead like he always did when presented with a conundrum. The arsenic poisoning made no sense.

Decker glanced at the ceiling, picturing its past; a perfect setting from which to embellish a legend, especially

He pictured the conversations to follow if he ever said what he was thinking. *"Tell us a story, Decker. Tell us about the hanging ghost lady who lives up the lane and poisons people."* For a cop, fantasy wasn't a sensible tool. He believed in logic, but there was none here. What kind of distorted, supernatural interplay had been conjured to produce this result?

A new element came into play. Decker listened. Was it the vague sound of laughter he was now hearing, or a maniacal glee of victory? He closed his eyes to center on sound rather than sight and try to reason it out. *Could the poisoned traveler have been a lynchpin to Marcy's past? Could a revenant have some sort of task to fulfill, and know when someone would reenter its sphere of existence?*

"Are you here, Marcy?" he whispered. "A dead woman who can bake up a pile of poison cookies?"

Straining the tenuous band between the real and unreal, he waited for an answer. When none came he considered climbing unstable stairs leading to the second floor, but what was the point of looking for something up a stairway, around a corner, along a corridor? He sensed that whatever was here walked alone. The light coming in from a window seemed to alter the surroundings, now eerie, unnatural... even grotesque. Holstering his weapon, he left the house the same way he'd entered.

The heavens had grown dark threatening one of those sudden storms that seem to come out of nowhere and pass just as quickly, appropriate to the setting somehow. A cool breeze rippled his shirt and trousers causing him to shiver. From the relative safety of his patrol car, he studied Marcy's house for what he hoped to be the last time. There was good news and bad. The good news: The house no longer beckoned. The bad? A figure stood behind a cracked windowpane, partially hidden in the shadow of a porch support. It appeared to be a young woman, her head canting to one side as if pondering something, or tilted from a twisted neck. The distance

was too great to read her expression. It could have been anything between a frightening grin and an unfathomable Mona Lisa smile. But Decker knew who it belonged to—the long dead Marcy come back to her home. For what? Retribution?

Or more likely. She never left.

His lips almost moved, but his thoughts sent a telepathic message, passing from one entity to another. *Guess you got 'em, Marcy.* Having a mind cluttered with ghosts and sinister shadows couldn't be allowed however. He was glad he hadn't navigated the second floor. Another partial quote came to mind: *There are more things in heaven and earth....* "Let sleeping ghosts lie," Decker murmured and drove down the lane in a murky drizzle that fit his mindset.

Jay stands on the side of the literary highway and thumbs down whatever genre comes roaring by. His storytelling runs the gamut from *Horror Novel Review's Best Short Fiction* to the *Chicken Soup for the Soul* series. His memoirs and essays report fact while his fiction incorporates fantasy, suspense, or humor featuring the quirkiest of characters.

150 Words About . . .
HOUSE OF DARKNESS (2022)

by James Newman ©2023

When you see Justin Long's name in the credits, two things are immediately clear: His character will be a smarmy douchebag, and said douchebag will die.

In *House of Darkness*, Long plays Hap ("short for Hapgood"), a smug young fellow who's picked up Mina (Kate Bosworth) in a bar, hoping to get lucky. But when they arrive at her creepy castle (!), things get weird. Mina's sexy, but more than a little "off". And there's someone else creeping around the place, just out of sight....

House is light on action and super-talky – if that makes you cringe like vampires cringe at crosses, you should probably avoid this one. But if you're willing to trust a good "slow burn" flick to pay off in the end, you could find worse ways to spend an hour and forty-five minutes. If nothing else, you get to see Justin Long bite it once again.

NOT TODAY ▭

by Zena Shapter ©2023

We're kept in what used to be a zoo. The larger enclosures are filled with transportation cages; medium pens are divided with taut wire fencing soldered into cells. Metal panel roofs shut out the daylight, and shut in the sweat-seeped stench of unwashed bodies. Beside each cell's door is a small data panel, fully integrated with dim downlights and the mechanical tentacles we were all so intrigued by at first.

Every morning the robotic limbs unlock our doors, empty our stinking waste buckets, leave a box of components for us to assemble that day, then prod us into a communal feeding area. Those caged along the border with the old elephant paddock say different enclosures are given different foods. I keep telling everyone it's nothing to do with supply – they're monitoring our reactions, our performance. I heard of a community locked up in an old gymnasium, all fed some kind of pink berry.

Died that night. Every last one of them.

"Andy?" I whisper, as I'm nudged along the winding passageway between cages. Underfoot, dead grass pricks and soft dung pellets suggest rats. The next tentacle's metallic tip presses firmly into my shoulders, catching a knotted curl of my hair. I grip against the twang of strands snapping, then overtake the person in front of me. Andy sleeps in a cage just along from mine. "Andy!"

Ahead in the line, his head towers above the others. He turns and smiles. A firefly in the gloom. Before *they* came, his would have been the type of smile that caught my breath.

"We need to make a stand," I hiss, my breath as foul as a carcass. "Don't eat what they give you. Tell the others."

His smile fades, replaced with an expression I know well. We all wore it those first few weeks: eyes wide, head shaking as if to say 'please god, no'. He slicks down grease-dark hair and keeps walking. "No."

"They won't kill us. They need us."

He doesn't answer, walks faster. Probably he thinks if he just does what he's told, he'll get through this.

I understand. Sometimes at night I dream of the home I once decorated with IKEA cushions and canvas prints of exotic beaches I hoped to visit. I'd put on special clothes to go out with friends searching for The One. My manager at the customer service centre kept promising to make me supervisor. But there's a time and place for hope, and this isn't it. Unless we do something, we're not getting out of here alive.

"Shh." A short woman in front glares back at me. Grey hair. Cavernous laughter lines caked in grime. A button nose red from crying. So those sobs last night were hers. "We *will* get out."

Did I say that last thought aloud? I shouldn't be surprised. This place, it takes from you.

"You want to see your family again?" I snap at her.

She narrows her eyes, keeps it all in.

We enter the shadowy cascade of rocks where lethargic tigers once leapt from level to level, then lazed around for visitors behind a now blackened sheet of glass. The wearied space echoes with our quiet murmurings, its limp air smothering like a barn of fusty hay. Scant downlights hum on their last breath.

Our nominated liaisons stand near the enclosure's only exit; beside them a wheeled cooler chest clouds with lemon-scented vapour. They hand out water bottles and food packages. Before the line can advance, a tentacle extends from the exit's data panel, examines each person's mouth with its tip. It has the grace of an orangutan and the precision of a dentist.

But it won't examine my mouth. Not today.

Andy parts his lips, obedient. Collects his package. Gives me a warning look. He makes his way to our usual rock. I want to follow him, climb up and suppose how this all happened, when we'll be released, what kind of world awaits us. But if we want our lives back, our planet back, we have to make a stand.

The grey-haired woman is next. She opens her mouth. Collects her water and package. Finds a place to eat.

My turn. "Just water today, please."

The liaisons exchange looks. Slow, like they've heard this before.

"Are you sure?" one says.

"It means you return to your cell," says the other.

Fine by me. If that's all it takes. I take the bottle and march back up the line, chin high. I want everyone to see: we have a choice. We can fight back. We're not their playthings.

Metallic tips usher me along, keeping me on track. Without the bustle of other bodies, each mechanical movement snikts louder along the passageway.

I stride faster, staying ahead, reclaiming my rights.

My cage is on a raised ledge, near an old internal viewing window. I catch my reflection in the darkened glass as I climb inside. Defiant. Proud. They can't take everything. This is just the start.

The door clangs shut. Locks. The tentacle on the door panel inverts and extends inside the cage.

I didn't know it could do that.

One metallic segment after the other, it reaches for me, aiming for my mouth. It wants its research from yesterday, from whatever experiment it performed.

I clamp my mouth shut and move back, hitting the window's cool surface. The tentacle extends further. I slink

sideways, hunker down, push myself into the corner that reeks with the foulness of my overused pillow and blanket.

The tentacle persists, its tip splitting into four flaps. I didn't know it could do that either. Inside the tip's opening, a smaller feeler extends, glistening. It quivers as if with excitement; then, with a sudden lunge, the four flaps grab my face and the tiny feeler slips inside my mouth. It tastes antiseptic, minty. Numbing.

I grip at the cage tentacle, pulling to loosen its hold.

It only clings tighter, clasping my cheekbones, my jaw. Inside, its feeler slithers over my tongue and down my throat.

I gag, drop onto my back. I want it out. Out.

It only plunges deeper, churning nausea.

I scrabble against the floor, tears seeping.

The appendage slinks deeper – down my esophagus, into my stomach, stirring, swirling.

I feel sick. I want to vomit. Reflexes jerk, stabbing with the urge to retch. My eyes squeeze tight from the sickening sting of it. I want to yell at them that I give in, shout for them to take whatever they want, just get this fucking thing out of my mouth!

All I can do is writhe on the cold rough ground, trying not to tense my stomach, because now the tiny feeler is stroking my insides, churning and twisting. Bile burns my throat. Tears drip. I clutch at my belly, my waist, anywhere the feeler moves in ripples under my skin. A larva in its cocoon.

More than that, it searches deeper, sliding into my intestines, curling with the stealth of a snake.

I sob, despite the hurt it brings. One twitch and the feeler could kill me. One nick, one slice – I'd bleed internally and spend hours dying.

Still, it moves, around and around, easing itself from intestines to colon, gurgling through faeces, pushing out air. It moves on and on – it moves all the way; it finds its way out, jabs a sharp hole through my pants. Exiting my body, it extends further – upwards, high enough to turn and face me, to regard me, long enough to know I've seen it. Then it continues through me to the cage door, wraps itself around a nearby bar.

With a firm grip, it straightens, raising itself, raising me with it.

Weeping in silent streams, I hook my feet around the larger tentacle, clutch and hold myself where it wants me to be. I breathe in and out, concentrating on the consuming agony, on just getting through this.

The feeler presses, moving from side-to-side, softly at first, undulating; then more and more until it's rocking me, swinging me. A hammock in a breeze. Its tip turns to watch, waiting.

I know what it wants.

I nod. I *am* its plaything.

Tentacle and feeler lower me carefully. A tiger with its cub. It unwinds from the cage bar, extends to the door panel, and merges into the metal. With a thunk, the feeler disconnects from the flaps at my face and slips down my throat to my stomach, squirting out a trail of minty liquid like a casual sip of water.

The flaps release me, close back into a tip.

I curl into a ball; one hand over my mouth, one at my stomach, feeling for the ripples to stop. Make it stop, make it stop.

The feeler takes its time, unwinding itself. It leaves me shaking, feverish.

It shrinks across the cage floor and disappears into the door panel.

The tentacle tip opens my door and waits.

I get up and walk slowly back to the others.

Zena Shapter is a multi-award winning author of science fiction, fantasy, speculative and contemporary fiction, conjuring journeys into the beyond and unusual. Author of *When Dark Roots Hunt*, *Towards White*, and co-author of *Into Tordon*, among others, she's a "writer with a need for adventure" (Midnight Echo magazine), creating "dark fantasy at its blood-soaked finest" (Australasian Horror Writers' Association), and "cold and brutal" (Tor.com) stories that "deserve your attention" (Lillian Csernica, Tangent Online). She loves movies, frogs, chocolate, potatoes, and living with her family on Sydney's beautiful Northern Beaches, where she's also an inclusive creativity advocate, writing mentor and editor. Find her online via @ZenaShapter and zenashapter.com

STRAND BABBLES

by Jeff Strand ©2023

Welcome to 2023! Wow, we made it! I know—I'm as surprised as you are! But I'd like to welcome you to this brand new year by getting all nostalgic for a few decades ago.

Don't worry, this column isn't going to be "Old Man Rants About How Things Were Better In Those Days." Because while I feel a deep nostalgia for going to my local video store, I can also clearly remember that I really, really, really wanted to see *Evil Dead 2,* and the goddamn movie was never in! I would ride my bicycle to the store every single freaking day, and it was always rented! Dammit! Argh!

So the days when I have immediate access to *Evil Dead 2* are superior to the days when I would lurk in the New Releases section, desperately waiting for the store employee to place a copy back on the shelf. Especially because one of the guys who worked there would mess with the New Release Lurkers and *pretend* that he was going to place a high-demand movie back on the shelf, and then feint and put back a copy of *Like Father, Like Son* (the Dudley Moore / Kirk Cameron body-switching movie that you haven't thought about since 1987, if at all) instead. That guy was a dick.

Still, there was the thrill of the hunt. I remember spending the summer with my dad and discovering that a video store near him actually had *Doctor Butcher, M.D.*! I may have squealed—it's been a long time and my memory is foggy. Do you know how long I'd been searching for *Doctor Butcher, M.D.*? Probably a couple of years. Not that long in retrospect, but a loooooooong time for a teenage horror fanatic. I was well into adulthood when I found a disreputable video store that had *Cannibal Holocaust*. It was a bootleg. These days I could get a remastered edition of *Cannibal Holocaust* from my neighborhood Best Buy or rent it online within seconds, but back then this movie was a dark secret, spoken of in whispers amongst my friends, and when I found a copy I almost—but, importantly, didn't—wet my pants in excitement.

I can still remember the adrenaline rush of those discoveries all these years later, long after everything I learned in school has faded.

Still, if I'd gone back to myself in those days and told Young Jeff about Shudder, he would've lost his freaking mind.

DIRT AS BOTH FIXED AND UNFIXED SHAPES □

by Andrew Giffin ©2023

The night after Grandpa died, he walked all the way home from the morgue. Mom heard the porch swing and there he sat, rocking in the evening breeze. His bare feet were all cut up, the trail of blood like a slug's. He didn't turn when Mom screamed.

We all came running, me and Dad and my older brother David. Grandpa stared into the distance, as if waiting for his Charonic rideshare. I looked away after noticing he was naked.

Mom cried, Dad holding her upright. She kept repeating herself, yelling "I don't understand! I don't understand!"

David called 911. He said later he didn't know what else to do. "We're at 232 Pine Street. We need...I don't know. My grandpa's back."

I can't imagine what the operator thought. 'My grandpa's back'. What kind of emergency is that? My wailing mother must've convinced the dispatcher, because two police cars soon arrived.

Officers stood on the porch as I gave my name, Louise Baker, explaining the swinging man had just died. One examined the bloody footprints leading off the porch and down the street. Another tried and failed to soothe Mom. Grandpa kept swinging, his gaze fixed on something unseen.

The ambulance took him to the same hospital where he died. We didn't go that night. No one said why, but I think we all hoped everything would return to normal. He's back where he belonged. This was all some kind of mistake-- they'd figure it out, and we could finish preparing his funeral. That's how our family treated problems--if you don't see them, you don't have them.

David and I slept in our parent's bed, under the guise of helping Mom. It did, but neither of us wanted to sleep alone. We became little kids again, not 13 and 16.

The hospital called in the morning. Dad left the room with the phone.

He returned with a grim expression. "They took his vitals, ran tests, all that. He's alive. They're keeping him for observation while they wait for labs, but they want us to come in." He looked at Mom.

"What happened?" She had barely slept.

"They're not sure. Could've been catalepsy from Parkinson's..." He trailed off after seeing the look on her face.

+++

We crowded in the doctor's on-call room at the hospital "for privacy about our sensitive issue."

"I want to prepare you for what you're going to see." The doctor rubbed the bridge of his nose beneath wire-rimmed glasses.

"Is it bad?" Dad said.

Mom's voice hovered above a whisper. "We watched him die. How can it be any worse?"

"Well, he's unresponsive so far, but not what I mean. I want to prepare you because his Parkinson's is gone." This took us by surprise.

"How is this possible? How is any of this possible?" Mom grabbed Dad's arm.

I tried to imagine Grandpa without the tremors plaguing him for the past eight years. In all that time, this was the longest we'd discussed it.

"We're still determining that--we have more tests after the first round. I want to apologize again for what your family is going through. False declaration of death is rare, but does happen."

"Doctor, no need to apologize." Mom stood. "There was no false declaration. My father died. He was dead, and now he's not."

The doctor didn't know what to say, so he led us to Grandpa's room. We pulled back the curtain. Grandpa lay beneath the covers, bandaged feet dangling off the bed as he still stared into the distance.

We stayed a few hours. Despite attempts at normal conversion, he didn't reply. My parents wordlessly decided it was time to leave, standing together. The silence lingered the whole way home.

We took the week off school. My parents sat us down and told us what the doctors said about catalepsy and false declaration of death--the party line. By the weekend Grandpa was back home with us.

He used his old wheelchair, wandering from room to room. I'd give a startled shriek after noticing him staring blankly from the corner. He never reacted. I spent a lot more time upstairs.

When I was younger I admired how he always joked around instead of letting his disease bother him. When he needed the wheelchair, his favorite joke became asking for a La-Z-Boy wheelchair.

That was his response when Parkinson's came up--joke until we changed the subject. Mom spoke this language fluently--together they taught the rest of us. Jokes were safe--we retold them the same way every time. Jokes as a ritual. Now I think of them as dirt covering the hole of things we didn't talk about.

His ghost came back to haunt us and everyone politely ignored him. His presence put us on edge, but we never discussed it. What were we supposed to do, kick him out?

+++

Two weeks later, Dad asked who kept tracking dirt through the house. David blamed me and I blamed David.

That night, the back door creaked open. I peeked out my window, thinking I'd catch David sneaking out. Grandpa pushed aside branches at the yard's edge, disappearing into the trees. I dropped, heart pounding, inching forward to watch him come back. *What's he doing?* I drifted off while waiting.

At breakfast I glanced at his frayed and dirty bandages. Grandpa always loved the woods. Why wait for night?

After eating, we scattered from him like roaches from the light. David and I headed to our rooms, Mom grabbing the laundry.

"Louise, can you help me with this?" Mom held a white basket overflowing with clothes.

"Sure, Mom." I followed her to my parents' room, sitting on the bed as she turned on the TV. We folded in silence, not daring to interrupt *Jeopardy!* reruns. I appreciated the distraction from last night. Grandpa stepping into the trees replayed itself in my mind. At least with *Jeopardy!* I understood the rules.

Mom grabbed one of Grandpa's shirts, her eyes glued to the screen. Dirt poured from the pocket, a small pile. Her eyes flicked down before returning to the TV. She added the shirt to his clothes, ignoring the heap on the bed.

She's choosing this, I realized. I thought back to the night Grandpa came back, our hospital trip the next day. Something I'd been too shocked to acknowledge clicked for me then--she acknowledged the truth, that Grandpa died. I scooped up the soil, hoping some honesty remained.

"What's this?"

"What's what?" Mom rolled a pair of socks together, very invested in Final Jeopardy.

"This dirt, Mom. Why is it in Grandpa's shirt?" I held it up to her.

She leaned around me, not breaking her line of sight. "I don't know, Louise, it's probably from one of his walks."

I wanted to scream about Grandpa walking into the woods last night, about how she knows he died. Instead I hesitated. Denial can permeate a home, like radiation.

It infected us. I wanted to resist, to tell the truth before becoming a carrier, spreading it to others. Parkinson's wasn't Grandpa's first disease.

"I can get the rest, honey. Go throw that away." She scrolled the TV menu, looking for another show. I headed to my room, sprinkling the particles behind me.

Over the next two nights I listened for the back door. On the third night, I decided to follow him. If Mom needed a shock to admit the truth, I needed more information.

Instead of going to bed, I snuck out the front door to hide in the bushes beside the house. From there I could survey the whole backyard.

As I waited, I thought about how the woods used to terrify me. Being in the backyard alone was my worst fear. I always felt watched from the depths of the trees.

Before the wheelchair, Grandpa took me on walks through the forest, showing me his love for silence. His passion erased my fear. I didn't have that luxury anymore.

Finally Grandpa crossed the lawn and entered the trees. I hesitated, creating distance but also working up my nerve. The seconds ticked by until my body obeyed my brain.

I sprinted until reaching the treeline. Grandpa crunched through the leaves ahead. I timed my steps with his and entered the woods.

After a few minutes, his sudden stop left my foot hovering mid-step. I eased into a crouch, creeping closer as a new sound filled the silence.

Grandpa stood in a clearing, his back to me, digging a large hole. The shovel bit the dirt, flinging it over his shoulder. He worked with a steady rhythm, an endless well of stamina. I found myself transfixed by his relentless pace.

He stood knee-deep in the hole, the circumference like a basketball jump circle. The misplaced dirt pile stood taller than me. *What's he doing?*

He worked his way across, nearing the opposite edge. What would happen then--would he keep digging, or discover me on his return to the house?

Shifting my weight, I readied my retreat. A branch cracked off to my right, deafening in the night air. Grandpa kept digging as I turned towards the noise.

Ice pushed its way under my skin as my heart flopped in my chest. Someone stood in the shadows near the clearing. I squinted into the darkness but couldn't pick out any details. They remained still. I told myself my imagination was trying to scare me. Even so I froze, eyes locked on the figure.

Grandpa reaching the edge of the hole drew my attention. I held my breath, but he only turned around to resume digging.

Before I could exhale, footsteps ran through the leaves to my right. Grandpa's head swiveled like an owl,

surveying my direction. The shovel kept working as he scanned.

I glanced back to the maybe-figure. It was gone. I cursed as my eyes searched the trees--coming out here had been stupid.

Grandpa's head straightened, and after an agonizing wait he approached the nearest edge of the hole again. When he turned his back to me, I ran towards the house.

I threw open the back door and ran upstairs, two steps at a time. Crouching beneath my window, I waited for him to follow. Forty-five minutes passed before he returned.

I climbed into bed, both thoughts and pulse racing. After dozing for a few hours, Mom woke me for soccer practice. Grandpa sat in the kitchen corner as we left, staring at the wall.

+++

I decided to talk to Dad. My attempt with Mom had been unsuccessful, but the burial instinct didn't come natural to Dad like it did with her. Maybe I could get through to him.

I waited until Mom went to the kitchen. I checked for Grandpa, but he must've been in his room. Dad sat on the couch reading the newspaper. I considered the best approach to bypass his defenses, running hypothetical conversations in my head.

"Dad, were you in the backyard last night?" I decided a fact-based approach worked best. The back door initiated this--best to start simple.

Dad flicked his newspaper towards himself, glancing around the room.

Mom stood at the sink in the kitchen, her back to us. She paused her dish-washing, her hands dripping at her sides. *She's listening.*

"Louise, gimme a hand in the garage, will ya?" He stood, dropping his newspaper on the couch.

"Sure." I followed him down the hall, past Grandpa's closed door to the garage.

He held the door open like an invitation to his office. I hit the light switch, illuminating the empty concrete space.

He peered down the hall before shutting the door. "What do you mean, Bug?"

"Someone's opening the back door every night. I checked last night and saw someone in the trees." *And it was Grandpa and he's digging a hole and something is <u>wrong</u>.* I wanted to tell him, but I didn't. Not yet.

Dad took a breath. "It's Grandpa."

My jaw dropped. He *knew?*

"I understand it's a shock, but remember, his...illness is gone. He needs walking practice."

"Okay, but...you don't think sneaking into the woods at night is weird?" I still couldn't believe he knew about Grandpa's nightly excursions.

"A bit odd, sure, but probably therapeutic for him. You know he loves nature."

The door opened. Mom stood in the entrance, her eyes darting between us. We stared back, kids caught by the teacher.

"Dinner's ready." She turned and walked back towards the kitchen. Dad followed a moment later without looking at me.

I stood in stunned silence at the extent of the rot. Why couldn't they just talk to us? David hadn't completely cut himself off, but for how much longer? Our parents were useless without undeniable evidence. I needed help.

After dinner I went upstairs and knocked on David's door. It opened a crack, strange electronic music floating into the hall.

"What's up?"

"Can I talk to you?"

He sighed and let the door swing open.

I shut it behind me, gathering my thoughts. "Okay, ever since Grandpa... came home, he's been different, right?"

"You noticed?"

I took a breath. "Let me start again."

"Louise, what's wrong?"

"You remember the other day, when Dad asked about the dirt in the hall?"

"Yeah..."

"That night, I heard the back door open. I looked outside because I thought you were sneaking out."

"I didn't-"

"I know you didn't. I thought so at the time, but instead Grandpa walked into the woods."

"Grandpa?" He sounded surprised. "You're sure you were awake?"

"I'm sure. I watched him the next two nights. Last night I followed him."

David's eyes widened. "Into the woods?"

"Yeah. He's digging a big hole out there." I waited for a response, but he only frowned. "This sounds crazy, but not any more than coming back from the dead."

"Did you try telling Dad?" He knew better than to ask about Mom.

"Yeah, right before dinner. He already knew--said the woods were therapeutic for him. I didn't mention the hole because, well..."

David nodded. He thought for a minute. "Show me."

"What?"

"Take me to the hole, I want to see it."

"I don't want him knowing we're back there."

"Fine, we'll go out front and down the street first."

We went downstairs, telling Mom we were going to the park to kick the ball around. After a few houses, we turned and entered the trees. From there I led David to the hole.

The shovel stood straight up in the center, the blade buried in earth. We surveyed from the edge.

"Why would he do this?" David said. I shook my head.

Next to us, the pile of dirt reached David's head, the outline of a person indented in the mound like a snow angel. I shivered, remembering the vanished figure.

"Something else happened last night."

I showed David the person-shaped outline, explaining about the figure from last night. His face darkened, the obvious unspoken: after Grandpa, what else was possible?

Light breaking through the trees caught a glint of metal beside the pile. Four other shovels littered the ground, muddy with handprints. We walked back in silence.

+++

That night I drifted off while waiting for the now-familiar sound of the back door. Instead the creaking stairs woke me up, the sky outside still dark. Motion-activated plug-in hall lights turned on, pouring under my bedroom door.

Twin shadows blocked the light, someone outside my room. I stared at them, waiting for the knob to turn, the door to open, but they never did.

I crawled to the floor, moving across the minefield of creaking floorboards to the door. With my ear against the carpet, I peered into the hall. Two dirty, bandaged feet stood on the other side. Grandpa, motionless and staring.

My breath slid heavy into my lungs. The full weight of my fear didn't register until I confirmed the feet were his. He stood in the open, where anyone could see him. I understand then--he doesn't care.

Resurrection wasn't his supernatural ability--it was denial. He denied death and formed scales over my parents' eyes--of course he stood there without fear or worry.

We remained in this stalemate until finally he bent over. I rolled away,

squeezing my eyes shut like I'd become invisible. He slid something beneath my door. I forced my eyes open and glared at it, not daring to move closer.

After an excruciating wait, he stepped out of sight towards David's room. I was desperate to lock my door but didn't want to risk the sound. Instead I shifted to examine what he slipped under my door—a small pile of dirt, resting on a dried leaf. I wanted it gone but didn't dare touch it.

With a tremendous amount of willpower, I picked myself off the floor and got in bed. I fell asleep eventually, watching the space under my door-- even after the hall light shut off.

In the morning my door stood open, his gift gone. I kept it locked after that.

+++

I told David about his nighttime visit, the dirt, about waking with the door open. David's door had also been opened.

"We have to do something about this." I sat on his bed.

"What can we do?" he said from his computer chair. "Mom won't talk about it, and Dad's trying to keep everything normal."

"I don't want him in our house. We don't know what he wants—what if he does more than open our doors next time?" I considered. "We need proof, something Mom can't explain away."

He nodded. "You've got something in mind?"

"I do. I've followed him outside, but I haven't done the opposite."

"Meaning what?"

"Have you been in his room since he came back?"

"No. He keeps the door closed."

"I want to look inside. I doubt Mom will go in the woods with us, maybe we can find something that'll convince her. I don't know what else to do."

"No, I think it's a good idea," David said, his face serious. "I think we should wait a few days, let things fall back into a normal rhythm."

In a few days, we'd go into his room. I suppressed a shudder and nodded.

+++

The next two mornings our doors were open when we woke up. We waited an excruciating two more days. That night, we waited for the sound of the back door.

I peeked out right as the branches swallowed his form. We went downstairs, David heading to the darkened kitchen to act as lookout.

Standing before Grandpa's door, I inhaled before unlocking the knob and turning it open.

A dirty room greeted me—literally, dirt covered the floor, dresser, shelves, the unmade bed. The empty wheelchair sat in the corner, the tires filthy. I hesitated on the threshold before stepping in Grandpa's footprints.

Underneath the mess, the ghost of Grandpa's room persisted. Crime thrillers and police procedurals on his bookshelf, photos on his dresser, jazz vinyls by his turntable--the remnants of his life, all buried in a layer of dirt. I lifted the bedspread to check under the boxframe, revealing tightly packed soil.

On the dresser, a framed photo of our family lay flat, small mounds rising from the surface, tiny shrines of earth. Dirt filled the inside of the frame too, between the photo and the glazing.

I turned to the closet and stopped. The floor there remained clear, aside from footprints to the door. I approached and opened it.

Five figures stood inside. I screamed. David's chair scraped across the kitchen floor as he came running.

"What the-?" He crossed the room. "Are you alright?"

I pointed at the figures--compact dirt, hardened with mud, leaves replacing clothes and hair. They were us. Myself, David, Mom, Dad, and Grandpa. The likeness shocked me, aside from one detail--the mouths on my parents' figures were missing.

"What the fuck," David said.

I nodded in agreement, my heart still pounding. I wanted to slam the door, leave this room, forget whatever was happening here.

"Oh my god." David leaned closer. "Did he run out of time on their mouths or something?" He examined our dirt parents' faces.

"Who's that last one? Him?"

We both stepped closer. Grandpa, naked like the day he walked home. We gaped, confused and disturbed. Something was seriously wrong.

"Is this enough to show Mom?" I said.

"Yeah, I think it's time to do that." He examined the dirt Grandpa, running a finger across the cheek. Its eyes snapped open and we both screamed.

The last sculpture was really him, his naked body coated in mud. Soil tumbled from his mouth, followed by a deep, raspy wheeze--a cacophonous sound from the depths of the earth. He grabbed David, spinning him into a chokehold. David kicked, his whole body twisting and thrashing to get free.

The replicas sprang to life, grabbing me, placing earthy hands over my mouth to muffle my screams. Grandpa dragged David from the room, followed by my captors carrying me.

Another dirt Louise opened the back door, allowing our horrific procession to pass before joining in. We crossed the backyard into the forest, where two more dirt families joined the march.

My initial disbelief thawed into yelling and kicking, squirming in their grasp. Clumps of their bodies crumbled where I hit them, the missing spaces refilling themselves moments later.

Branches whipped my face as our small crowd followed Grandpa through the trees. We reached the clearing, stopping at the hole. Darkness obscured the bottom--it had become a pit.

Grandpa stood at the edge as three dirt Davids grabbed the real David. Grandpa directed dozens of replicas. They climbed from the hole like ants, depositing dirt before descending again.

My captors carried me towards Grandpa and David. I went limp, becoming dead weight. As we neared him, I lunged, freeing my arm to push him in. My fingers brushed his shirt as he stepped out of reach. A horrible thought occurred to me as I stared into the pit: *I'm going to die and come back, like him.*

I screamed then, screaming for help, for Mom and Dad, screaming obscenities. The figures regained control, my dirt mother's hand covering my mouth again. Grandpa leaned forward with a finger to his cracked lips.

"SHHHHHHHH." He hissed like some ancient reptile. Dirt obscured his gums, the resulting darkness an imitation of the hole.

He spread both arms, like a crucifix, and replicas scrambled out of the hole. They clamored over each other in a mad rush, crushing the smallest and slowest. These fell away in crumbling chunks, their dismembered, still-moving limbs revealing thin, twisted skeletons of gnarled branches.

The last few climbed free, crowding the edge. The ones holding me and David brought us close to Grandpa--close enough to see his pallid, discolored skin, to smell the rot underneath. He leaned in and kissed my forehead.

I recoiled from his dry, cracked lips, but the replicas held me tight. He pulled away, peppering me with dirt, before repeating with David. The replicas set us down in front of him.

I turned frantically to escape, but the dense crowd blocked the way. They radiated outward in concentric circles, ours pressed against the edge. Grandpa stood behind us in the next circle as David and I faced the hole.

Warm, stale air wafted up from unseen depths, carrying the smell of wet, rotting earth. The dirt figures stood motionless, awaiting orders. They reminded me of a photo in school, warrior statues in some old tomb.

Grandpa put his hands on our shoulders as a Louise beside me stepped into the hole. They followed around the circle like dominoes, plummeting into the darkness. As the wave approached us, Grandpa's grip on our shoulders tightened, and I realized with horror his intentions.

"David, he's going to push us in!" I pulled away even as he reached around to hold me by the neck.

David struggled beside me as the wave reached us. Grandpa and his circle stepped to the edge, pushing us off.

We screamed and slid over the edge. The replicas built handholds into the walls of the pit, and we grabbed on, our feet dangling over the depths.

"Just hold on!" David shouted. The next row of figures began their wave. I stared up at Grandpa, who gazed down at me with a grin of filthy teeth.

His smug smile transformed my fear into anger, an acidic disgust at his version of family culture. We didn't speak with each other, couldn't be vulnerable with each other. Without that, what made us a family? He made us strangers instead. I hated it.

My screams became words. "Why couldn't you stay dead? We were better off, and you couldn't even let us have that! I thought you came back wrong, but this is the real you--emotional void, black hole sucking up all of us until nothing's left but the things we don't say. Go back to the dirt, they're your real family."

The figures paused halfway around the circle, my words echoing through the trees. I'd never been that honest, not out loud. Even then, dangling from the hole, I felt embarrassment, shame. *What's David going to think? What if my parents heard me?*

The ground rumbled, some of the still-frozen figures falling in. Grandpa leaned forward. At first I thought he wanted to watch us fall, but his smile evaporated, his whole face drooping into the expressionless mask of his Parkinson's.

"He's changing back!" I shouted.

From the depths, a gargantuan arm rushed past us, surfacing into the night. The hand hovered above Grandpa, its skin sickly and pale, an almost-translucent white the color of maggots. It absorbed moonlight, pulsing with a nauseating glow.

It emanated wrongness, the opposite of life, moving with jerky motions like an old silent movie. The death he denied, now here to reclaim him. I had weakened his hold on it, enough for the dirt to fall away and the natural order to restore itself.

The fingers wrapped around Grandpa, his head poking between the sagging fingers. As the hand retreated into the hole, he gazed into my eyes. His restored Parkinson's froze his blank expression until he disappeared from sight.

The rumble subsided. My breath escaped in ragged gasps, my insides fluttering. Our doppelgängers crumbled back to dirt, losing any remaining form without Grandpa animating them. Dirt flooded over the edge as they collapsed.

David pulled himself up first, offering me his hand. We stood and brushed ourselves off, catching our breath. The woods were quiet, circles of dirt surrounding the hole. I stepped towards the edge and peered inside. He was gone.

"What are we going to tell Mom and Dad?" I asked. David only shook his head. We stayed for some time before going back.

I started a shower, eager to get clean. The sight of muddy handprints produced shudders as I undressed. I caught my reflection, my dirt mother's handprint centered perfectly over my mouth, Grandpa's lips outlined on my forehead. I stared until steam obscured the mirror.

Grandpa didn't come back this time. Mom and Dad didn't mention his absence. We all silently agreed not to bring it up. A weight lifted from everyone's shoulders--especially Mom. She started smiling again.

I had resolved in the shower that night to tell my parents everything, to open the floodgates. Her smile changed my mind. What right did I have to take it away? It was over, why bring it up again? Best to bottle it up, bury it. I can live with that.

We kept his door closed. It became a room in our house we didn't go into anymore. I wondered if it was still covered in dirt.

A few months later, I went back out to the clearing. It all felt like some strange dream. The hole was gone. Filled in. Grandpa's wheelchair sat where the edge had been. How it got there, I don't know. I decided it was David and left it at that. Probably him that filled the hole in, too.

Satisfied with my chosen answers, I turned and walked back home. I didn't go out there again.

Andrew is a high school English teacher from Richmond, VA, where he lives with his wife and two daughters.

He is an autistic author whose most recent work can be found in Planet Scumm, The Dread Machine, and Abyss and Apex, among others. He has a passion for doom metal and solo tabletop RPG's.

150 Words About . . .
WATCHER (2022)

by James Newman ©2023

Don't confuse it with that Netflix series. This is the *Watcher* you should watch.

The always-wonderful Maika Monroe (*It Follows, The Guest*) plays Julia, who recently moved to Bucharest with her husband Francis. Although their marriage is a good one, Julia feels like she's on the outside of the world looking in, as her hubby works long hours and she struggles to learn the country's language. Oh, and some dude keeps staring at her through the window of an apartment across the street...a guy who might be the serial killer who's terrorizing the city. If only people would believe poor Julia – including Francis, who's supportive one moment and infuriating the next! – instead of treating her like a child with an overactive imagination.

I expected a *Rear Window* rip-off, but *Watcher* is one hell of an unsettling thriller. Hard to believe it's director Chloe Okuno's first feature film. Watch it, man!

THE MAIDEN IN ROBES

by Christi Nogle ©2023

Grandma always had a lot of what Bill called cooter-plants growing in the greenhouse back behind the ponds, but we paid them no mind. When we kids first came to live with her, she told us we were not to touch anything back there or else. Other kids might have taken that as a challenge to enter the greenhouse and touch all the things, but not us. Our grandma was mean as could be, and we did not cross her. I never even knew the word or why the plants were called cooters. We only ever saw them through the dappled greenhouse glass, so they just looked a little like flame shapes.

There were a lot of other things in the greenhouse that we never saw up close because we were obedient children. I suppose our friends always thought it strange how we grew up without any piss and vinegar. Never a spanking, never the need. We *were* docile, maybe a little fearful, but not maimed in the mind or anything like that. Grandma was fair; she set her limits and we obeyed.

How do you keep children from wandering into the road or jumping into the river? You tell them not to and show them how serious you are, and they by and large don't do the terrible things you fear they'll do. Well, Grandma was the same way; there were just more things she was serious about. Never lie, cheat, steal, and so on, but also:

Never go into the greenhouse.

Never bring anyone home without permission.

Never go up the stairs. Those are *Grandma's* rooms.

Never cross Grandma—with your words, with your mind. Don't get in her way. If she's headed past you, step aside.

Respect and boundaries were what it came down to. It was easy enough to be good with rules so clear, and the four of us grew up strong and good and kind. My cousin Bailey married young. She made a fine mother. Cousin Bill went into fixing people's houses. He isn't married yet, but we hear his work praised all around town. My brother Henry was supposed to work with plants, like Grandma, but he became an apprentice to the baker and has a little sweetheart named Emily. Grandma would like them to live here when they marry, but they'll want a place in town I'm sure.

I'm the baby, but now I'm twenty, old enough to have a sweetheart of my own. Absolom Eugene Underwood the Third, possibly the most eligible bachelor in the county, the light of my life! His people are not happy about this match, but his money is his own. I wonder what he sees in me except I'm sweet. I hope that will be enough.

We have permission to sit on the front porch, so that's what we do. I gaze into his piercing eyes and hear of his education, his travels and adventures, all his wants. I'd say he's censored things for the benefit of one so innocent, but one day *we* will travel, we will adventure, and everything long concealed will open up for me!

+++

"We'd like to walk around sometimes," I tell Grandma. Eugie's so full of life he gets restless sitting all the time.

"Walk where?" she snaps. She washes dishes so tensely I'm afraid she'll break a glass. I watch the water for blood.

Nervous, I clasp my hands. He hasn't told me just what to ask for, so I say, "We might like to walk around the pond."

"Your idea or his?" she says.

"Mine," I say quickly. I hope she won't see how I flush with the lie.

She rocks back from the sink, dries her hands. She looks me up and down. "You sure? I think that boy tells you what to do sometimes, no?"

"No," I say, going redder with the lie and with indignance. If she didn't want me obedient, then why on earth did she make me this way?

Maybe she is the only one I'm ever meant to obey? No, it isn't that. She wants me happy like all the rest of them are. Eugie will make me happy. He's the only thing that will.

+++

The ponds are unlovely, but it feels good to walk. The damp between our clasped hands unnerves me so much I can barely focus.

Eugie points and asks, "What are those?"

I say "Grandma's cooters."

He's stunned for a second and then he laughs deeply. He drops my hand to shield his eyes for a better look past the greenhouse glass.

"Just some old cooter plants," I say.

"Why, that they are," he says. His mouth twists as it often does, like he'd like to laugh some more right away but shouldn't. He takes my hand again, and on we go.

I'm glad. I never have liked the greenhouse. I have a memory from long ago—maybe when Mom and Dad and my aunt and uncle were all still alive—the greenhouse filled with smoke or mist. Glowing, anyway, gray-white against the starry night.

+++

Family dinners are rarer now. Usually it's just Grandma and me, but tonight my sweetheart shares our meal.

"What are those flowers called, those pink and brown ones in the greenhouse?" Eugie asks. I do not mention that I've already named them to him.

Grandma pauses, wiping her lip with the napkin, then says slow and clear as if every word is its own pearl on a strand: "The Maiden in Robes."

I do not cross her by correcting, or asking, or anything. I hope that the conversation will veer elsewhere, and it does. We speak of Bill's construction projects, Bailey's children, Henry's early hours and the magnificent loaf of bread he left for supper.

I wonder when I'll have anything of my own, but I do have something. I do.

Eugie squeezes my knee under the table when Grandma's absorbed in her pie. I nearly choke, fearing she'll see, fearing and relishing the strange action of my nerves whenever I'm touched by him.

+++

"No, we can't," I say.

"How will she know?" he says.

"It doesn't matter whether she knows. What matters is that it's forbidden."

He looks at me as though I've raised in value. That's all well and good, but he *will* ask again next time. It's all he seems to think of now.

Respect and boundaries. When we marry, he'll be the one I obey and vice versa. For now, it's still Grandma's house and Grandma's rules.

+++

"You have permission," I say when he arrives on the step. I didn't expect to feel sad saying it.

Eugie pauses, looking stunned. Maybe he wonders what I might be granting permission for. I'm suddenly aware of sweat between my crossed knees.

"I asked, and she says you can," I say. I nod gravely toward the ponds and greenhouse.

"Well come on, then," he says, reaching for a hand. I don't reach back but fish in my apron pocket for the key and pass it over to him.

"*You* have permission. I have to stay here."

He will stay here, then, if I can't go. We will make distracted talk on the porch with his eyes all out of focus until I say, "Please. Really, just please, just go." He will go and come back more quickly than I expected, but he will be flushed and will hurry off toward his car too soon. I will have to call him back so he can give me Grandma's key.

I'll think he's going to be back soon and pester me for it again, but he doesn't come back.

+++

The Maiden in Robes is not a pretty flower. At its best, it's just a flat flame, like a single spike of bromeliad, and yet those who encountered it in the field spoke of its great beauty. I read a few of these descriptions much later, in a library in the country where this plant once grew wild. I was completing research for a book, something I'd have never imagined doing when I was young. But that was half a lifetime later, or so it seemed.

Only one firsthand account remains, but the secondhand tellings confirm that the flower looks like a lovely woman shrouded in heavy robes or blankets with only perhaps the curve of her head sticking out near the top.

She moves under the burden of the coverings. She struggles to open them, and you strain and struggle to see.

Your eyes are so heavy looking at her.

She says if she has one night with you, she'll be real. Though swooning, you're ready for it—about to burst your skin.

The longer you look, the more of her you see—and the further away she appears. She had seemed a Thumbelina right up by your nose, and now she's a full-sized woman far in the distance. Nearly free of her blankets now. . .

+++

We haven't left the house in ages. I'm restless from sitting and from the lack of sleep.

"He's never coming back," I say. I can't hold in my tears anymore, so I turn away from Grandma.

"He is," she says.

"He isn't," I say, and I get a strange chill. *Never cross Grandma.*

But she is not angry when I turn back. Her face is soft and sweeter than it ever was before . . . and frightened.

Someone who's chastened herself realizing she's gone too far. She says, "He never left, not really."

My eyes focus past her to the starry night beyond the windows. I turn and, weeping, climb the stairs. *Never go upstairs. Those are* Grandma's *rooms.*

I am searching for the key. Digging in pockets and crashing things to the floor. These rooms are nothing special, nothing different from what's downstairs.

She is speaking. I don't catch it all.

Your house now, soon enough. Your rooms, your rules.

Take the key.

I can't find it.

Take it all.

Hate me if you will. . . only stay.

+++

If a single flower can bring a man to ruin, what could a few dozen do—and in a closed-up space, besides?

I anticipate the white-gray glow before I come upon the greenhouse. What happened here long ago? My parents and Bill and Bailey's mother—this must have been not so long before they passed. And then why can't I remember why they passed? All three of them ill or injured for a time, it seemed. They were somewhere else. We weren't allowed visit.

I wish I could bring it all up, but once I'm at the door it's all I can do to throw the rock and find the inside handle. In the gust, I see the maidens. They look just like me. They do look far away and lovely. They're calling to me, but there's something else too. Mist, I thought, and there is something more. A web? Not fine as spidersilk but more like a lacy sponge.

"The Bridal Veil," an awe-filled voice says right behind me.

The veil's tendrils catch on me before I swoon. I fall, and Grandma catches me.

+++

Boundaries. Respect. They're mine now. I say what happens.

She sleeps downstairs now. Eugie and I sleep in the same room but separate beds. No one would see if I climbed into his, but it wouldn't be right. We'll wait for Grandma to bring the preacher. He'll probably have to come upstairs, as we're too weak just yet to go anyplace.

We'll rest up and feel better soon, or I will. Eugie already feels quite well. Though he can't yet walk or speak, his face rests in perfect bliss. When I come back from the bathroom in Grandma's robe, his eyes track me. His lip trembles. That is all.

I've been picking the bits of veil-root out of him a little at a time. "An hour or two a day," I say, "and we'll have it all done by the wedding."

Today it's the leg all bumped up like chicken-skin. It's a beautiful leg. He's a beautiful man, still. He manages to look like he has his wits about him, and I think the illusion will hold up even when he speaks. I don't know how bright he was, really, before.

"We can still travel. We can still have adventures," I say. His money is still his own. No one will cross us.

I'm tweezing out a spike large as a cat's fingernail when he flinches, making me leave a little tear in his pretty skin.

"Don't do that," I say, "Don't move."

And he doesn't. The rest of the night, he does not move.

Christi Nogle is the author of the novel *Beulah* (Cemetery Gates Media, 2022) and the forthcoming collections *The Best of Our Past, the Worst of Our Future, Promise*, and *One Eye Opened in That Other Place* (Flame Tree Press, 2023). Her short stories have appeared in over fifty publications including PseudoPod, Vastarien, and Dark Matter Magazine. Follow her at http://christinogle.com and on Twitter @christinogle

INTERVIEW WITH JOHN URBANCIK

by Rick Hipson ©2023

John Urbancik is a dark fantasy author of over a dozen books and numerous short stories. He's also an amateur photographer who is willing to try anything at least once to create the perfect shot or story idea. His work includes the six book DarkWalker series, Inkstained: On Creativity, Writing, and Art, The Corpse and the Girl from Miami, and La Casa del Diablo. While Urbancik's primary desire is to draw out our curious wonderment from every mysterious corner of the world and beyond, he's also never been one to flinch at an opportunity to seduce us into the sort of dark places we would otherwise never dare to venture into.

At the end of a grueling stint of ghostwriting to pay the bills, John unleashed a well of ink which had been pent up too long and was finally allowed to spill as free as blood on a battlefield. I recently sat down with John in-between his ink letting to discuss his newest novella, his best advice to new writers, brand new yet to be revealed book news, and whatever else might incriminate the two of us as we explore what fuels his muse and learn why we need to pay attention.

Considering I just enjoyed the hell out of your recent release of La Casa del Diablo, it probably makes sense to kick things off by asking you, how did this fantastical western of dark cosmic adventure come to be?

La Casa del Diablo came from the ghostwriting. When I originally got the gig, I had to do an audition piece, a five thousand word start of a novel. The first five thousand or so words of *La Casa del Diablo* were the audition piece for the ghostwriting gig, but I switched it up a little bit and I made it, you know, weird.

I couldn't imagine if I'm reading, say, the first quarter of a book and then just saying, "This is pretty amazing, I can't wait to find out what happens next, so I'll put it aside for a year." I imagine that must have driven you bonkers knowing the book is there waiting to be finished, waiting to see where those characters were headed.

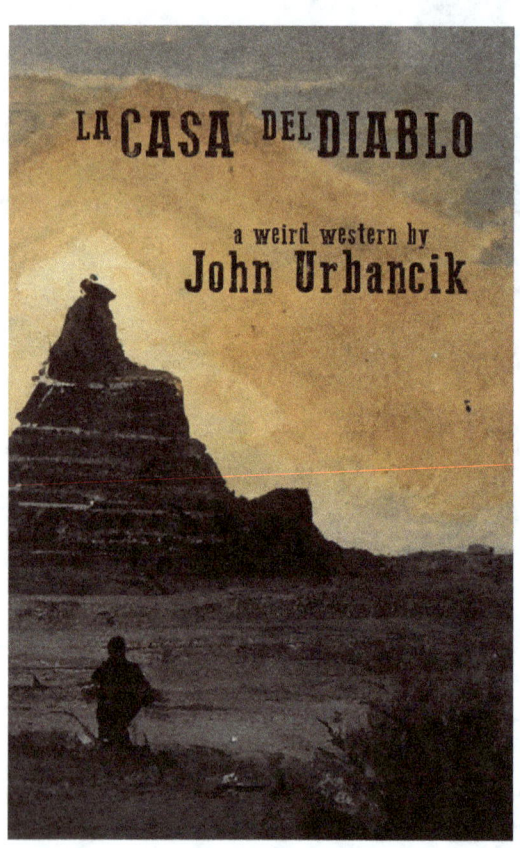

Well, it served a purpose. It got me the ghostwriting gig, and I needed the money then, and I probably need the money now, but I don't have it now. But it served its purpose, and at the time when we stopped doing the westerns and started doing the fantasies, I moved. I'm in the middle of Pennsylvania now. I thought, well, I've got a little bit of free time, let's see where the rest of this book goes. I thought it would be my final western, and then I ended up doing another four more for the ghostwriting thing.

The ghostwriting had parameters and had particular needs or particular things that needed to be done. Whereas this, the *La Casa del Diablo* just needed to be me, and it really is. It really becomes me. It's definitely my version of a western.

One of the most impressive things for me in *La Casa del Diablo* is you can almost view it as a two-act play. The first half is very much a western while the other half takes a turn for the dark and fantastic, yet the story never quite strays from its western roots. Was the blending of both elements something you had to plan out in advance of the writing?

I don't think I had to think of it that way. I mean, the characters are who they are, and they have to stay true to themselves essentially for the entirety of the story. It's not like I can have 'em do anything that would not be appropriate for a western because he is a western character. He just deals with the unusual in the way that I would think Clint Eastwood would deal with the unusual if he faced it.

If I may touch upon the ghostwriting gig one last time, I'm curious how you managed after being so immersed in another writer's world over the course of thirteen books, but then had to let it go with nothing else to do with it. That must be such a strange butterfly transition.

It's a little bit complicated. I was grateful to have the work, and I put everything I could into 'em, but they were never my stories. I as a writer, as an artist, have a compulsion to do the work. I can't stop. If I were never to publish another word again, I would still be writing until the day I die. I don't have a choice. The ghostwriting didn't count. It didn't help that. I still had the urge, the yearning to do my own stuff. I just didn't have the time or the energy to do my own stuff. While I was happy to have the work, when I stopped doing ghostwriting, I immediately started doing my own work again. I would say emotionally, psychologically, it was the biggest benefit to me. This is why we have *La Casa del Diablo* and *Amusing Curiosities*. This is why I'm working on the follow up to *Sins of Blood and Stone* and a follow-up to one of my other novels. This is why I'm also working on putting out my vampire novel. I guess that's news. Nobody knows about that yet.

Nobody sparkles in it, right?

Nobody sparkles, no. No, it gets very dark, but it uses a couple of different types of vampire tropes. You see Anne Rice had a big influence on me when I was young. There's also the Nosferatu style vampires in there as well and the mindless, blood-drinking beasts called vampires because what else are you going to call them?

Sure.

But they're not the same thing. They're not the same, and I might as well tell you more. The project is called *Vampires in Madrid*, or *Vampires of Madrid*. I always forget what preposition I use, but it asks the question: Why aren't there very many stories about vampires in Madrid? What stops the vampires from being in Madrid? You've got stories about vampires in Paris, Vienna, Rome, New Orleans, New York City, Boston. You've got vampires all over the world.

Yup, even in Pennsylvania.

Yeah. But I was not able to find very many that even touch Spain. I was living in Spain when I asked this question.

A fair question to ask. Would I be a little bit out of my realm here if I were to ask you what was the answer you came up with? Or is that what the story as a whole is; the answer?

It's integral to the story, and I couldn't tell you now. But what I can tell you is, again, mixing the genres; it's part that and it's also part romantic fantasy with time travel elements in it.

In a way the two stories merge, and honestly, it's the story of my experience in Spain. I lived there for most of nine months with my partner and that is where she got diagnosed with cancer, and just a couple of weeks after we left Spain, she died. That experience, the entire experience, the good, the bad, is all in that book. I'm a little afraid to start because I know I was in a dark place when I wrote it, and I felt at the time it was probably the darkest thing I've ever written. I'm going to have to go and find out for sure because I can't just say, "Here it is." I must go through it and make sure everything in it is right. I must do this revision. If I'm going to self publish this, I'll have to do the layout, and everything is just going to be me diving right back into it.

Do you think it helps separate the emotions more if you're doing all the technical stuff yourself, or would you rather give the nitty gritty publishing work *to somebody else*?

I don't know if it can help me emotionally anymore in that way because I think that kind of emotional work I've done, we're talking about something that happened a little over three years ago.

Right, not that long ago.

Not that long ago, and honestly, it's not completely done. She wrote a book herself, and it is just about to come out.

It's called *The Disney Animation Renaissance*. It's basically the history of the Disney Animation Studio in Orlando, and I got copies of that in the mail about a week ago.

Oh, that's gotta be bittersweet.

Yeah, you know I cried. I wasn't expecting that. So obviously the emotions are still there. But because writing is the way I've always dealt with everything, I think I could go into the story again and make sure it's right and clean it up, not to do more emotional work, but because I've already done enough emotional work to get in there. And either I'm right or I'm wrong, you know? It could be that I'm in tears every night again and that won't be fun or easy, but you know I'm still going to do it 'cause what choice do I have? I don't. I don't have a choice. I told you that before. It's a compulsion.

That's the power of writing as well as reading, I suppose. You can't know exactly what's going to hit you, when it's going to hit you, how it's going to hit you, until you're there. Maybe that's a good thing. Maybe it gets stuff out

that you didn't realize was swimming somewhere down there under the surface until it's like, oh, hey, there's some light to move towards and come out of.

Yeah, it's a little early to be talking about that though 'cause I still have other things I'm working on that will definitely be out first such as *La Casa del Diablo*, *The Museum of Curiosities*, and a few other things, including a book from Eraserhead called *Echo*.

Oh, I hadn't known about Echo.

It's a mixing of genres. Erasherhead does bizarro stuff and it's probably the most bizarro thing I've written. It is essentially a story about magic, about a stage magician who finally does some real magic and switches places with his reflection in a mirror. His reflection doesn't live the same life that he does because, although he has the same skillset as the stage magician, he is a professional thief.

And now they've both switched places, and so it becomes an interesting story. It's actually a novella, and it's the first of five tightly interconnected novellas that make up a book called *The Secret History of the Palace Theater*, which is a book that I haven't sold and I haven't got any expectation of releasing any time yet. It is a mixture of genres because there's fantasy, there's creation myth in there, there is cosmic terror in there, and magic. Lots and lots of magic.

John, to switch gears a bit, I want to ask you about The Writers Bootcamp retreat that your pals Brian Keene and Mary SanGiovanni have taken over from Tom Monteleone and F. Paul Wilson. I understand you're one of the instructors for next year's iconic event. Regarding writers who might be wondering what they could be doing wrong, what they can improve on as far as their craft goes, to even qualify to be a student of the bootcamp, are there any commonalities of being a beginning writer where someone might feel they've got a great story, or maybe they've got a great idea buried in mediocre writing which can be improved upon, that you see a lot of writers getting wrong?

This is going to sound weird, but mechanics is important. The way you tell the story and the way you write the story. As you go through, and when I was young, when I was starting, I would do a revision of my story and those first times, it was like, "Alright, I got to remove the word *that*," because ninety percent of the time, *that* is extraneous. It doesn't mean anything. *He said* that *it was cold*. Well, why doesn't he just say, "It was cold"? Or better yet, why not just shiver or something? There are better ways of doing certain things, and some of it is, for me, a little bit about the musicality of it, the way that it sounds and the way that it works. The mechanics play directly into that. I think a lot of younger writers, and I don't mean this as a generalization, I don't mean younger people who are writing, but people who are beginning to write no matter what age you are, haven't mastered the mechanics yet. They're not entirely familiar with how to say what it is that they want to say in the clearest and most concise ways. They sometimes get in their own way. I've done some editing work for a variety of people, and a lot of times the edits are simple edits. It's remove the word *that*, remove the word *even*, remove the word *suddenly*. Like *suddenly* nothing. *Suddenly* means it is already not sudden because I had to get through that word.

Good point.

There are ways of making it seem sudden without having to say *suddenly*. If you have to say it, you haven't done it right. And I don't think that's a problem. You do that in the beginning because everybody has to start to get through that. I know I did. I'm sure in my first stories: new sections were begun with the word *meanwhile,* or *on the other side of town.* You don't need to do that, but it's a matter of knowing how to do it and knowing what needs to be done. After the first rounds or revisions, and when I finally stopped using *that* in that way, then I found there were other things I was doing consistently which needed to be changed. And then when I fixed that, there were other things. There's always something else. There are still things today. You're always going to have those words that you fall on as a crutch to get through.

Those pesky fillers.

Those fillers filter into the writing in different ways. *Very* becomes a filler word. *Really* becomes a filler word. *That* became a filler word. When you start working through those you find the stories become more tightly written. When you can tell your story more tightly, then even an idea not wholly original can be better told and can become interesting. A big thing with beginning writers, writers at that earliest start and steps of their career, is they just need to write it. Write through the crap. I heard, what was it? Everybody has to write a million words of crap before they can write something good.

That makes sense.

I was definitely thrilled when I counted the words in *InkStains*. That by itself was over a million words.

That's a helluva lot of stains.

Yes, and I had been writing novels for decades before I did that.

Well, here's to decades more of your dark, beautiful magic, John. It has been an absolute pleasure chatting with you as always, my friend.

NO MORE STRINGS

by Brian Hornfeldt ©2023

Many years ago, there lived an Italian puppeteer named Geppetto, who made his living carving wooden puppets and marionettes. He traveled his hometown performing for children leaving school and tired parents. Geppetto did what he loved, but after a time, the money began to slow, and the puppets began to wear. Children no longer cared to see him perform, and the puppets, once his muses, now judged Geppetto in the darkness of his workshop, whispering amongst themselves the failures he brought upon himself. Nobody understood how Geppetto felt. How he *really* felt.

Nobody except Pinocchio.

Geppetto set down the quill, stretching his arms into the air, before leaning down to examine his work. He reread the passage he had just finished, worried his play wouldn't sound enough like the stories from the children's book he had purchased. Glancing over his shoulder, he locked eyes with Pinocchio, sitting motionless on the counter above him. The puppet perched like a Gargoyle atop a grand church, a visage of evil meant to frighten those who beheld it.

He looked back at the paper and read it again.

"I've just finished the first part of your play, Pinocchio," Geppetto said. "I think it will be the greatest of the year. The children will surely let you—" the words choked in his throat. The air grew cold as Geppetto turned his head. Pinocchio was now inches from his face, suspended by strings that stretched to the ceiling, seeming to disappear into the infinite black void that hung like a cloud overhead. A drop of sweat formed on Geppetto's forehead and ran gently down his spectacles. The puppet hung and stared. Unmoving.

Pinocchio's mouth swung open, and Geppetto flinched from its abruptness, bracing for what was to come. Words fell from the puppet's hollow orifice as if weighted with lead, snaking through the air, forming tiny snowflakes as they traveled to Geppetto. He held his head away, trying to prevent them from entering his ears.

*This play **must** be the greatest. We have no room for mistakes, Papa. You must do this for us. For me.*

Geppetto's body was wracked with chills, tremors spread down the length of his chest before resting in his stomach.

"Of course, Pinocchio. Of course, it will be... It will be." Frost formed around the lens of his glasses, providing him momentary relief from the wooden boy hovering before him. All that bled through the white haze were a pair of shining black eyes and the void within its mouth. He shut his eyes tight.

Clock's ticking, Geppetto.

He held his breath as he opened his eyes. Pinocchio was back on his perch, observing. He breathed a ragged sigh of relief and placed his head in his hands, tears welling in his eyes. *What have I done to deserve this torment,* he thought, wishing someone would hear him and answer. But, as always, the thoughts remained his own. He brushed the tears from his eyes and began to work again. *Clock's ticking,* he thought to himself, wringing his hands as he tried to force the words into his mind. But the words wouldn't come.

An hour passed, broken by occasional scrawls from Geppetto's quill. He couldn't help sneaking glances at Pinocchio, who remained motionless with the other puppets. The void above had thinned, and with it went his fear. The ceiling began to show through the darkness as the workshop returned to itself. Thoughts of the past seeped into his mind between brushstrokes. The time before Pinocchio felt like a dream. A serene bliss when it was him, and only him. The dream changed as it drew closer to the present, becoming bleaker, marred with the knowledge of what was to come.

Though, hard as he tried, Geppetto couldn't recall *how* Pinocchio came to be.

Surely he had carved him, as he had carved the rest, but the memory evaded him. There was only the before and the after. The in-between didn't seem to exist. He tried to think harder, sifting through memories in search of *something.* And for a moment, there was a light—a brief image of himself holding the wooden boy, surrounded by absolute darkness.

DONG. It was gone, and his feeling of recollection was fading faster with each chime of the clock. Geppetto cursed under his breath and stood up, careful that Pinocchio wouldn't hear his swears. He remembered what happened last time, absentmindedly rubbing the small scar on his forearm as he left the workshop. The clock stood alone in the foyer, the seconds ticking in tandem with his footsteps as he passed.

Geppetto climbed the staircase with quickened step, looking over his shoulder to ensure Pinocchio wasn't following, and entered his bedroom. He bolted the lock and exhaled, unaware he'd been holding his breath.

Climbing into bed, he pulled the blankets over his head and cried. The faint moonlight painted silhouettes against the bedsheets, and to Geppetto, they seemed to point at him and shake. He could imagine the laughter racking the featureless figures and cried until sleep came and silenced his sorrows.

+++

Gripping the script tight, he removed Pinocchio from his rack, careful not to tangle his strings in the process. "The play is finished Pinocchio," he said with a plastic smile. "Soon, we'll perform for the town. Are you ready to start the rehearsals?" The puppet lifted its head from Geppetto's hands, the chill setting in once again.

There isn't much time, Papa. We must hurry. This body cannot contain me for much longer.

You're lying, Pinocchio. Geppetto thought to himself. *Your body is fine. You want to become a real boy. There is nothing wrong with you now.*

He imagined Pinocchio reeling from his words. The coldness surrounding him dissipating, as hairline cracks scattered across his wretched body. He saw the puppet clutch at its crumbling pieces, before shattering across the floor. After a few moments, the cracks began to fade, and the puppet rested in his hands. The chill in the air returned. Geppetto's hands began to shake.

The children must hear the play, Papa. We must bring them all to listen.

Geppetto shuddered at the thought. He knew Pinocchio; what he'd do if someone misbehaved. But the children in the city *were* delinquents. His thoughts drifted back to a time before Pinocchio, when he still traveled the town to perform. He'd find his cart tipped, puppets smashed or stolen. Other times they'd come to jeer at his performances. Once, a group of teenagers had shoved him to the ground and stolen his days' wages. How would Pinocchio react to this at his play?

You're a coward Geppetto. The puppet crooned. *The children will know better than to misbehave when we arrive. I'll be sure of it.*

He had almost forgotten Pinocchio's favorite trick. Without hesitation, he changed his thoughts to the play, Pinocchio's dazzling performance, uproarious applause as they begged for an encore. Though a tinge of fear lurked beneath. Had he been listening when he thought about his demise? He couldn't think about it now, but he hoped for his sake that he hadn't.

The rehearsals began the next day. Pinocchio's fluid movements startled Geppetto at first; he had never seen him this limber before. His joints turned smoothly, realistically. Everything about him felt real. *Maybe you* are *a real boy after all, Pinocchio,* he thought, stifling a laugh. But the strings glinting over his head ruined the illusion. He'd asked Geppetto many times to cut them, but something inside warned him against it.

Cut my strings, Papa. Free me. I want to play with the other children.

The words crept into his mind. Pinocchio's dance slowed to a halt. Had they come from the puppet, or had they been in his head? It was becoming harder to tell the difference. He rubbed his eyes and Pinocchio resumed his performance. Sunlight poured through the windows, bathing them with its rays, though the heat was negated by the never-ending chill radiating from the puppet's wooden body. Geppetto glanced into the hall and looked at the time. 6:15 PM. Only 45 minutes until his work shift ended.

Pinocchio had established a schedule for Geppetto when he appeared. This was one of the earliest memories Geppetto could conjure of Pinocchio's arrival. 7:30 AM work began, 7:00 PM work ended. There were no days off and he wasn't allowed breaks. The callouses on his fingers had just begun to heal from the quill sores he'd gained from weeks of endless pressure.

Days of rehearsal continued, and Pinocchio's movements grew more graceful. On the tenth day, he seemed more akin to a professional ballerina than a monstrous wooden puppet.

Though only on the outside. Geppetto knew all too well what he was capable of when he didn't get his way. As Pinocchio finished his final routine, Geppetto applauded his performance (with a twinge of fear, though he wouldn't allow the puppet to know) and asked him for another take, with a little more speed on the final number.

For this, Pinocchio had taken part of his ear.

If he hadn't lived so far from town, the neighbors would have heard him howling. A guttural, ear-piercing scream. Pinocchio's speed and agility were unrivaled, only impeded by the strings attached to his body; the one structural weakness that limited his outbursts. Geppetto often thought of what he might be capable of without them.

As Geppetto struggled to staunch his bleeding ear, Pinocchio settled atop his stomach and grinned, licking the blood off his jagged fingertips. The boy began to lacquer his body and strings with the crimson fluid, coating himself in a thick, sticky layer. Geppetto watched as the wood absorbed the blood, leaving no trace. He saw the strings fraying near the edges, the tight restraints weakening. With each outburst, Pinocchio came closer to freeing himself.

+++

Geppetto couldn't tell whether the chill in the air was from a coming cold snap, or Pinocchio's excitement as he sat atop the rickety cart. Auburn leaves dotted the path as the hill crept down towards the city. The old puppeteer had been through days prior, spreading the news of his return. It had been a year and three months since his last performance, and a year since his last journey to town. Many he visited admitted they thought he had died.

Word spread fast; Geppetto could hear chatter as they inched closer to the crowd. For a moment, he forgot about his wooden master clattering loudly on the cart beside him. He forgot of his throbbing ear. He forgot his scarred arms and legs. His chill replaced with a warmth that seemed to seep from the crowd like a heartbeat.

Pinocchio's strings fell from the cart, next to Geppetto's hand.

The crowd was not to know of Pinocchio's living self. He was to play the role of the puppet and Geppetto the puppeteer. As he held the cross bar, the strings stretched around his fingers, securing them to the wooden grip. The show would end when Pinocchio was finished, as he had been told many times.

Lifting the wooden boy from the cart, he gently lowered his legs to the stone floor. He stuck the sheet music he had written into the self-playing piano, fastened tight against the back of the cart. Pinocchio's legs quivered with excitement as the first tune began to play.

His motions were perfect. There wasn't a single deviation from the original rehearsal. The music seemed to flow from his arms as if he were conducting with his movements. The lines Pinocchio delivered drowned the noise of all else, enchanting the audience

The rest was a blur. Blood. Children screaming. The knife peeling flesh like the skin of a potato. Pinocchio covered in the dismembered pieces, trying to perfect his form and become a real boy.

I am complete Papa. Only one thing remains...

Then came the cold, but this time, it was followed by darkness.

+++

Sunlight soaked the courtroom in a hazy yellow veil. Geppetto's wrists were raw from the iron cuffs secured around them. The judge sat high on his seat like an eagle eyeing its prey.

into a deeper and more intimate trance. Geppetto was so focused on the performance, he barely recognized the strings were inching their way up his arms and down his chest.

As the music swelled with the final verse, Geppetto felt his arms being drug into the air towards the cart. The strings bound him to their whims, reaching his hands into the repairs compartment on the side, his fingers clenched around the hilt of his carving knife. He began to panic. Blood dripped down his arms, the strings cutting into his skin as he fought to free himself from the bindings.

Geppetto's mind was empty. He felt numb. Pinocchio sat on a table on the far edge of the room, near the judge's podium. He could hear murmurs and sobs from the crowd gathered to watch the trial. A woman called him a monster between her tears. A man said he'd give Geppetto the same fate he'd given those children. The town was somber, but lively. All eyes rested on him as he stared silently at the puppet on the table. He drifted back to the case as the prosecution asked for his defense.

He was silent for a long time. Thinking. The words evading him once again, as they had so many times before. Images came to his mind, as he sorted his thoughts into cohesive statements. He wanted to start somewhere. The beginning? There wasn't much beginning to explain. He tried to remember how it all began.

The memories erupted like a burst dam.

The ocean. A woman in blue sitting on the sand, watching the waves crash in the distance. He offered her some company, and she accepted. The air growing cooler as their conversation turned from pleasantries to something more personal. The waves climbing higher, engulfing their ankles, and grasping for more. He told her how he wished for a son. How his days felt empty, and he was losing his reasons to keep going. The waves submerged them, but he didn't notice. The stars painted their constellations against the water around them. She told him she was magic and could grant his desires if he wished. He closed his eyes and wished. Then the void. Pinocchio's soul being torn from his own, molded by the darkness he was submerged in. Pain. A hideous feminine laughter emanating from the tar-like sludge that had once been him. Then, he was home. A wooden boy lain on the table beside him. Pinocchio.

"Your honor. The defendant is clearly unwell. I move to have him committed and serve life in the infirmary."

He heard the judge's cool agreeance. The uproar from the crowd, the judge's gavel. The chill had returned. He could feel it. Feel the ice forming beneath his palms, feel the iron contracting around his wrists, tightening their grip. Then he saw Pinocchio gliding across the evidence table towards the knife. He saw the puppet shudder with anticipation. Saw his jagged hands wrap around the blade. The strings. The strings. The strings.

He felt an urge. Memories of the lie coming back into his mind. He could feel himself screaming, telling Pinocchio that he lied. He had wanted to be one with the children, not kill them. They were dead because the boy had lied.

The gavel crashed; the murmurs grew louder. He could almost see Pinocchio growing as his words emboldened him. He saw the black eyes gleaming towards him, his mouth curling into a dark grin.

Pinocchio's arms opened, tracing a wide arc towards the shimmering restraints. The bloody boy grinned with delight. Freedom at last.

Geppetto couldn't move. Couldn't speak. Time slowed to a crawl as the knife cut the strings. Then a sound, piercing through the freeze and frosting the spectacles across his face.

Freedom at last, Papa.

Brian Hornfeldt lives in North Carolina and attends the University of North Carolina Greensboro. He is currently studying for a major in English, and a minor in Creative Writing. This is his first publication.

150 Words About . . .
BAD MOON (1996)

by James Newman ©2023

Based on a sadly-unknown novel, this flawed but fun werewolf flick was helmed by Eric Red (*The Hitcher*).

Single mom Janet (Mariel Hemingway) is surprised when her n'er-do-well brother Ted (Michael Pare) shows up at her front door. It's been years since she saw him last; now he wants to reconnect with Sis and her boy, Brett.

No problem! Janet's stoked to see her brother. Her German Shepherd doesn't trust Uncle Ted from the start, however. Must have something to do with Ted getting munched on by a werewolf while he was away doing God-knows-what.

Aside from some yucky CGI (oh, how you set the bar forty years ago, *American Werewolf in London*), this one's a solid monster movie. Watch it, then read the book (*Thor* by Wayne Smith)...just prepare to cough up hundreds of bucks for a copy of the OOP hardcover on Ebay. The paperback ain't much cheaper.

WE ELECTED A DEAD MAN

By Andrew Kozma ©2023

It was unexpected when the dead man was elected mayor, but understandable since he'd only died two days before the election. It only made sense that many voters wouldn't have realized, their attentions spans numb to any event that didn't directly impact their lives. But this didn't make it any easier when the mayor showed up at your door—at *my* door—to personally thank me for my support.

"The only reason I came back is because I was elected," the mayor slurred, a maggot dropping from his mouth. The antenna of some insect wiggled from his ear. "So, thank you for your support."

"Oh, you're welcome," I said. "You're welcome."

"Please accept my congratulations!" His syllables mushed together with his torn rag of a mouth. He extended his hand clumsily, like it was a dull knife, and his fingers waggled uproariously, each of a different mindset.

I didn't take his hand.

"Accepted, Mr...mayor. There's no need for all of this."

The man's name escaped me. I hadn't voted for him *specifically*, I just checked the box of the first name on the ballot, in a hurry to do my civic duty

and get out of there. I don't like people, I must admit, though I don't admit it to anyone directly.

The mayor's hand hung in the air like a dead fish. The mayor waited for me to shake his hand, motionless as a pile of dead fish. It was early morning, the sun was just making itself a burning coal in the sky, and the mayor smelled ripe and looked like he'd be more than willing to ripen all day on my front steps, if so needed.

His hand felt loose when I shook it, the skin of the hand moving apart from the bones. I'd read before of people's hands being gloved, so damaged by burns the flesh just slips right off, and as I let go of the mayor's hand his skin seemed to hold on to mine, a sandpapery burr, and acid spurted into my throat.

"I hope—" the mayor started, then had to stop. He wrangled his tongue in his mouth, the tip of it peeking between his lips as if trying to escape. "I hope you will do your part to help our fair city. Join a committee. Help find new homes for stray roadkill."

"Yes?" I said, unsure what I'd actually heard.

"The more bodies we have, the better," the mayor said. His teeth were strangely perfect, probably fake, and his bloated face was absent of wrinkles. Up close, he looked like every badly-lit politician on TV. He was dead, but could I blame him for that? Should I hold him to a higher standard?

Some of his hair tousled itself in the breeze, one of the strands of hair falling out to squirm on the concrete steps. A

worm. It squirmed towards the house and I let it through the door. I didn't want to be rude.

"I'm not sure what I have to offer," I told the mayor. His eyes were cloudy and I'm not sure how well his facial muscles worked, so his expression was frozen in what I took to be friendliness. "I'm not very political."

When I began to close the door, the mayor put his swollen foot in the way and the squish of it made me let go of the door entirely, allowing it to swing open so the sudden rush of air brought in the mayor's rotting perfume. Or had he stopped rotting? Was he now frozen like this, at the stage of death he was in when elected, preserved as such as long as he remained in office? He winked at me, his eye rolling loose in its socket.

"We are all part of the body politic." The mayor flopped his arm to take in the entire street. "See how many are willing to help make this city the best city in the country?"

Up and down the street were people dressed up in suits and dresses, shambling from door to door with purpose. My neighbor across the street had apparently tried to flee in their electric car, now motionless on the asphalt, surrounded by a mob of the mayor's supporters. Dark things lay on the ground around the car. Lost shoes? Was that an ear? I looked away.

"You can pick up litter, for example?" the mayor said. Was his voice getting clearer, or was I just growing used to his strange way of speaking, like his mouth was full of dirt? "Or canvas for change?"

"What kind of change?"

"The best kind!"

Something tingled in my ear. I felt a nub of flesh on the inside of my cheek. I roughed it clear with my tongue and spat it into my hand, a tiny grub squirming like a newborn baby. The mayor's death-clouded eyes looked on with pride. My skin suddenly felt like an ill-fitting suit. The heat from outside had wandered in and make me feel crisped like chicken rind baked in the oven.

"Am I okay?" I asked the mayor, fear worming in my gut.

He handed me a clipboard and a list of names, some of which I recognized from the obituaries. A fly buzzed onto my hand, then my face, then up my nose. I couldn't object, so I didn't. The mayor poked me in the stomach.

"What you feel in your gut isn't fear," he said. "It's patriotism."

Andrew Kozma's fiction has been published in Escape Pod, HOAX, The Dread Machine, and Analog. His book of poems, City of Regret (Zone 3 Press, 2007), won the Zone 3 First Book Award, and his second poetry book, Orphanotrophia, was published in 2021 by Cobalt Press. You can follow his writing on Patreon (https://www.patreon.com/thedrellum) or on most socials as thedrellum.

LA CASA DEL DIABLO

review by Rick Hipson ©2023

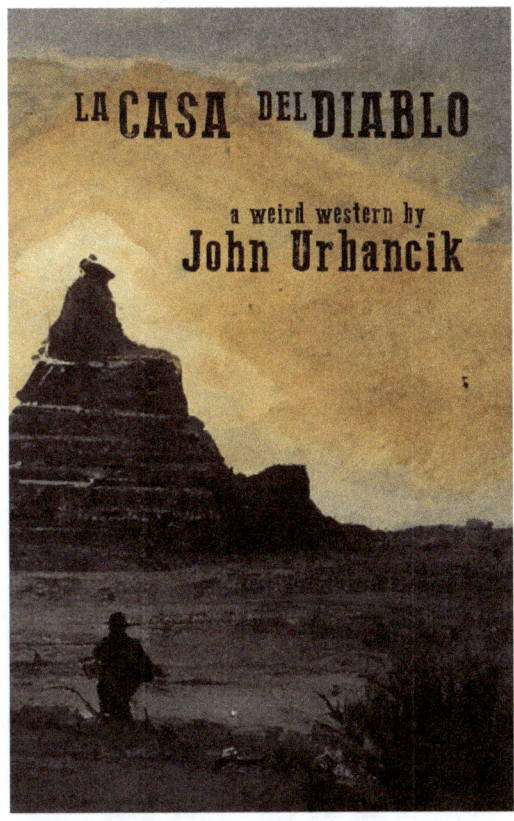

Title: La Casa del Diablo

By: John Urbancik

Published: 2022

Publisher: Dark Fluidity

Pages: 124

A master of dark fantasy and mythical wonder, Urbancik proves how the magic of otherworldly chaos can be found in the most ordinary places. Traversing the dusty plains of New Mexico Territory, Urbancik fires off each word and detail with deadly accuracy.

Utilizing the untamed environment to perfect execution, we're introduced to a lone gunslinger named Kasper Diehl who rides his horse across the desert, hell-bent on avenging the murder of his family. For twenty years, the guiding light of Kasper has been fueled by a vendetta to hunt down the good for nothing sumbitch who killed his parents and sister before his eyes.

With his horse and his father's Walker Colt as his sole companions, Kasper comes across a scene which gives him pause and, in time, would alter his trajectory in unimaginable ways. A stagecoach sits as if abandoned with its horses and coachman clearly dead. Emerging from inside is a beautiful young woman and an older gentleman she calls *father* who claim bandits had recently come upon them while they hid out of sight. Kasper easily catches up with the bandits nearby and after returning to the coach with assurances their safety is in order, the grateful duo invite Kasper to settle in with them. As luck would have it, they happen to be headed to the same derelict destination known locally as La Casa del Diablo, a renegade town built upon the sins of those with nowhere else to go.

Reaching their destination, standard Western tropes peel away, allowing Urbancik's signature blend of alchemy to bleed into the lives of his characters and that which lay before them. Parting ways with the young woman and her *father,* Kasper seeks out the killer responsible for putting his family in the ground. What he finds instead is something born of fantastic nightmare which threatens to throw him from his war path and destroy life on Earth as he knows it. Kasper must decide if he is the hero he never asked to be while somehow putting to rest the ghosts of his past.

In a world where the good guys don't often win, this novella is a classic example of the extent which desperate men, both good and bad, will go to when destinies collide within a maelstrom of apocalyptic consequences.

Saddle up and ride out for a fast-paced hybrid adventure of cosmic proportions not soon forgotten.

www.ingramcontent.com/pod-product-compliance
Lightning Source LLC
Chambersburg PA
CBHW081214170626
46811CB00010B/3281